LJ
JK
RM

P9-CAY-819

# Kato's Army

Wells Fargo Agent, Jay Kato, didn't want the job of taking a consignment of gold to Green River Springs. The town held too many memories – bad ones.

His cousin, Duke Heeley, had threatened to kill him if he ever came back to town, but he put aside his misgivings when he was offered a generous bonus. After all, he only had to deliver the money to the marshal.

However, when the time came to step off the train, a hail of bullets greeted him. Kato knew then he'd have to raise an army to fight them all.

ſ

# Kato's Army

D.M. Harrison

A Black Horse Western

ROBERT HALE · LONDON

ISBN 978-0-7090-9192-9

Robert Hale Limited
Clerkenwell House
Clerkenwell Green
London EC1R 0HT

www.halebooks.com

Typeset by
Derek Doyle & Associates, Shaw Heath
Printed and bound in Great Britain by
CPI Antony Rowe, Chippenham and Eastbourne

# CHAPTER ONE

'Only one more job, Kato, that's all I ask,' Putman said. 'A short trip to Green River Springs.'

'Can't you ask someone else?' Jay Kato looked slightly irritated. 'Surely I'm not the only Wells Fargo agent available?'

The distinctive sound of a Colt .44 and a belt loaded with lead bullets echoed off the walls of the sturdy adobe building as it clattered on to the table.

Like anyone with a reputation as a top-class Wells Fargo agent, Jay Kato needed a huge personal armoury to sustain that image. However today was different. He looked like a man in mind to quit.

'I'm tired of getting shot at,' he said. As he sat down he took off his hat and held it out towards the man opposite. 'See that?' He pushed his finger right through the crown. 'I plumb near got a hole in my head.' He put his hat back on. 'I come here to give you notice. That was my last job for the company.'

The man he spoke to, Brendon Putman, took one look at Jay Kato and considered, correctly, that he had an almost impossible task in persuading him to do the job he had in mind.

Brendon Putman couldn't argue with that. There were other men. But he wanted Kato. He was a good man to have in a difficult situation. Although whether he could risk telling him that every other agent he'd sent to Green River Springs hadn't managed to deliver the money was another matter. A few had taken a bullet and returned in a wooden box. In the light of Kato's next comment, Putman decided to keep the information to himself.

'You know I don't want to go back to Green River Springs,' Kato said.

His face looked older than his twenty-eight years, like it had a lot to say, but only the brave or foolish would ask him to tell the stories that had shaped it.

For a few moments the two men sat without speaking in the agency situated off Main Street in Rock Creek, Wyoming. The place had grown from a few log cabins and a general store to a thriving town since the advent of the railways.

Wells Fargo shared the building with the telegraph office and the sound of the tap, tap, tap of the operator was the only thing to interrupt the silence between them. Then Putman cleared his throat noisily.

'Well, it's not exactly going back,' he explained. 'You're just dropping a hundred thousand dollars off at the station.'

The man paused. Even to his ears it sounded unbelievable. Kato's flint-grey eyes bore into him. The other man tugged at the collar round his fat neck, as if it was getting hard to breathe inside the room.

'Well, no,' he said. Jay Kato's unflinching gaze made him admit a bit more of the truth. 'Marshal Lessard will be there to meet you and escort you and the money to the bank. Job done.'

It sounded more than neat to Jay Kato. It sounded as if Brendon Putman was trying to pull the wool over his eyes.

'So nobody is going to try and take this money off me? I will have a nice train journey, nip quickly into the bank and come home again?'

Brendon Putman placed the palms of his large thick hands together as if pleading with the other man.

'Maybe not,' he agreed. 'But if there is trouble I think you will be the right man for the job.'

Kato pushed the brim of his California-style hat further up his head, uncovering his thick blond hair, as he whistled through the gap in his teeth. He pushed the chair back so it balanced on two legs.

'So that's it,' he said. 'No one else wants to go?'

Brendon Putman stood up and walked around the room.

'Look, no one knows there'll be a hundred thousand dollars on that train. Marshal Lessard is not going to announce the fact. And if it stays that way there will be no problems.'

He sat down again, agitated. Wells Fargo agents operated all over the United States guarding valuables. Jay Kato had a reputation as an ace agent. He always delivered. That was why he was in demand.

'There's a chance the information will get out?'

Kato missed nothing.

'The money is important,' Putman explained. He avoided answering Kato's question. 'The town is growing as the railway expands and investment means more of everything for everyone.'

'If it's that important you should send an army of men with it.'

'A discreet journey with one man will be the most effective way. But take anyone you want, Kato, if you feel better doing it like that.'

Jay Kato allowed his chair to swing back to rest on four legs. He opened his mouth to speak. He didn't want this job and was about to refuse, but Brendon Putman thwarted him by his next statement.

'There is a matter of a golden handshake, so to speak, with this job,' he said.

'How much?' Kato asked.

'Name your price,' Brendon Putman challenged.

Kato thought hard about his answer. He'd been an agent for four years following a spell in the army.

He'd joined the United States army to fight Indians. He'd seen them as the enemies of the white man. The pioneers conquered the West and in doing so came into conflict with the red man. At first the pioneers had been welcomed for the trade and the guns and whiskey they brought with them but, like everything, the trading had its down side. The white man killed the buffalo. These creatures roamed the land and had provided food, clothing and currency for the Indians for centuries. Unfortunately these great beasts also took the grass the white men wanted for their own cattle, and encouraged the Indians to remain on land the incomers wanted for themselves.

Kato saw another side of the picture as he spent four years in the army. Disillusioned, he left and ended up in the Wells Fargo outfit. He felt it was an easier job guarding money and greenbacks from being stolen by outlaws than trying to keep Indians on reservations.

'Ten thousand dollars,' Kato said. 'On top of my fee.'

He rose to his feet, sure that the sum named would be rejected. Such a sum would mean he could buy somewhere to settle down. He didn't want to be travelling across the country when his bones creaked and his hair turned grey.

Brendon Putman held out his hand. 'A deal,' he said.

The reply left Kato puzzled. There had to be an angle to this. Why would anyone pay $10,000 to have this money delivered?

Questioned closely by Jay Kato, Brendon Putman explained why someone wanted to get the delivery through safely.

This shipment wasn't the first to be sent to Green River Springs, but it would certainly be the last if it didn't get to where it was intended to go. The railways wanted to invest all along the track, build up towns that people wanted to live in. They'd need supplies delivered and eventually their folks would visit. It wouldn't be like years ago when people went off to the West in wagon trains and, once they'd waved goodbye, relatives and friends in the East never saw them again.

A ranch manager, Lloyd Braddock, amongst many others, had built up spreads covering thousands of acres over the years and, thanks to the railways, now shipped beef to the north and east of the country. Braddock also rented out land to cattle owners waiting to ship their beef. Now with the threat of the rail companies diverting their tracks to safer territories, he feared his empire might crumble.

Jay Kato shrugged. It was an easy way to get rich, he thought, especially if he went alone and the 'golden handshake' was only for himself. He'd seen a few gunmen off and he was prepared to take a few more out if they got in the way of his task of ferrying money from Rock Creek to Green River Springs.

Putman watched Kato leave and gave a sigh of relief that the man had accepted the job. And Lloyd Braddock had given him a little more than $10,000 to get this job done. If it turned out well, his pockets would be lined with gold as well.

# CHAPTER TWO

'We'll be arriving at your station soon, sir,' the conductor said. 'The next stop, sir.'

Jay Kato pushed his hat up to look at the man he'd asked to let him know when the town came into view. The conductor touched the peak of his cap, almost taking a bow towards the man seated in the last wagon of the Union Pacific train. He showed due respect for a loner who'd insisted on having the whole of the wagon to himself.

A half-smile crossed lips that murmured 'thanks'. Kato's flint-grey eyes, briefly stared up then he pulled his broad-brimmed felt hat back over his forehead and they were hidden once again.

The conductor took it that the audience was over and went away.

Kato's posture appeared relaxed but still guarded, gave him the air of someone ready to take on whatever life handed out. A man who'd experienced many things, not all of them pleasant. He wore the blue-grey pants of a soldier, with a brown buckskin jacket over a blue flannel shirt because it was practical and comfortable. He liked the army boots, long enough to tuck his pants in, and comfortable enough to wear for a month without taking them off if he had to.

His army service had been short and brutal; the military took all they could out of him and threw him back again. Now he took on the role of a Wells Fargo agent, moving from town to town, and instead of fighting soldiers or guarding prisoners he fought outlaws and guarded greenbacks and gold pieces.

Jay Kato noticed people called you 'sir' when you packed iron. So he always sat with a gun across his lap when he travelled. He stroked the walnut grip of his trusty Colt with its long cylinder and slim barrel. It had been his friend for a long time. It meant he didn't get any trouble.

The company he worked for sure didn't treat him like a gent, though. He shuffled around on the wooden slats that served as a seat to try to get comfortable. It cost $110 to travel first class from Omaha Nebraska to San Francisco. Not that he was going that far, which was just as well as he'd only been given twenty dollars travelling expenses, so it was third class only when he bought a ticket.

There was a lot of money to be made now that the railways had opened up the world and made it smaller. The days of the wagon trains, stagecoaches and steamers were numbered as people chose to take four days, four hours and forty minutes instead of four months to travel from east to west: that is if you didn't mind buffalo herds moving slowly across the lines, the train robberies and the Indian attacks.

Slowly he stood and stretched and rubbed his butt and decided he didn't think it was a whole lot more comfortable travelling by train. Out of the window he saw the rolling countryside, dotted with sage bushes and the cottonwood trees and willows that drew the line of the Green River. He could see the backdrop of the White Mountains with ponderosa pines against the skyline and felt he'd come home.

He wondered what sort of welcome to expect. Folks had long memories and in his case, they weren't all good ones. He turned away from the wooden window frames, thinking that maybe one day they'd put glass in the darn things, and sat down again. He checked his Smith & Wesson Colt again to make sure it was loaded. He knew it was because he'd spent most of the journey doing just that, as well as checking the Winchester repeater rifle he carried at his side. That good old Yellow Boy he never let out of his sight, 'cause it cost him forty

14

dollars to buy. He wasn't looking for trouble but he was prepared, for his own protection and to guard the money he carried.

The train whistle blew as it pulled into the station. The blue-painted monster with its red wheels and yellow wooden carriages eventually came to a halt in a cloud of steam. Jay Kato, with his guns, jumped to the ground and the conductor helped push the bags out to him.

The town, sprawling out from the train lines, didn't boast much of a station. It was a forgettable place, consisting of an old train wagon divested of wheels standing alongside a ramshackle log pen whose board roof was covered with sod, and whose windows had no glass. At first glance it looked to Kato like the town definitely needed all the investment the money he carried could buy.

He heard the train whistle blow its fierce sound again before the engine dragged its load towards the next stop. He watched as the conductor frantically waved his flag as if glad to be rid of him, but far too savvy to say that to his face. Kato decided that was too fanciful a thought probably due to the heat of the midday sun frazzling his brain. He was the only passenger who'd left the train here. Later he wished that, like all the other passengers, he'd had the sense to continue onwards to find somewhere more civilized.

Jay Kato turned and looked towards town, where

he had to carry his burden of heavy bags. Suddenly it looked a long way away.

The town of Green River Springs didn't seem like there was much to it at first. Hitch rails ran all along the street in front of false fronted buildings, inside which every necessity of life was stocked. The stores catered for essentials such as liquor, cigars, dry goods and clothes. Alongside these were the marshal's office, the bank and the telegraph office. They stood majestically, towering above the other buildings, as if keeping an eye on things. On reflection the place was solidly built with the Green River and the rail line running parallel with each other before spreading outwards. The town had the potential to spread right into the White Mountains, which would provide a natural defence on its other three sides.

Putman had told him that Lloyd Braddock was aiming to build stockyards by the rail lines to house all the cattle before they got transported out to the north and east of the country. The town would be permeated with the odour of beef, but to most that meant the smell of money.

Some towns disappeared as if in a puff of smoke, left as ghost towns, but this one looked here to stay. He knew that further down the track Bryan Town in Sweetwater County had flourished until its river dried up and people had moved out. Perhaps that was the reason this place had started to do so well.

But robberies and general lawlessness were threatening its stability. However, outlaws could be brought to justice more easily than a river could be made to flow again.

He thought of the saloons and the red-light district. He knew the area well because he'd often frequented the Lone Star saloon in his youth. He thought of Lilly Chester and wondered whether she was still there. On lots of occasions he'd paid for her to dance with him and it had cost him all his month's money just for one evening in her arms. Dave Partridge, the saloon owner, discouraged this; he'd lost too many girls to marriage that way. Lilly was different, a high-class lady, but she said she wasn't the marrying kind.

He'd expected Marshal Todd Lessard to meet him at the station. That was the arrangement as far as he knew, but he decided to make his own way and not wait around with the baggage he carried. First he wanted to find himself a horse or a lift because the bags he'd guarded all the way from Wyoming to Utah seemed somehow to have become heavier under the heat from the midday sun. He turned towards the uninviting buildings to find out whether anyone was there, but the only thing that greeted him was the pinging of bullets off the wheelless wagon and the log pen.

A jagged spurt of earth a mite short of his boots as it hit the ground left him in no doubt that he was the target.

His hands went to his guns and he replied in kind as, almost in the same set of actions, he dragged the bags to the log pen. The bullets dogged his footsteps, threatening to catch up with him. Luckily the door stood open; had it been closed he'd have gone straight through it. He wasn't about to stay and become a shooting target for someone as crazy as a kicked racoon. Quickly he closed the door behind him and moved to the centre of the log pen as the shooter got the distance right and the bullets plugged into the door.

He knew he probably wouldn't win a prize as the most popular guy hereabouts but he didn't believe he warranted such a welcome. Nobody other than the marshal was supposed to know about his valuable cargo.

Then he recalled a recent letter which he was carrying in his top pocket, from the marshal's daughter, Blossom, and thought about what she'd written. She'd warned him not to come back to this town. Duke Heeley, fresh out of prison after serving his sentence, had sworn to get even with the man who'd cheated him out of the proceeds of a bank robbery.

And the worst thing was, Jay Kato had written back to tell her that he was on his way in the near future, and to look out for him. He hadn't said he was on a job for Wells Fargo, but if she'd mentioned it to Heeley, maybe he'd put two and two together and come up with $100,000.

# CHAPTER THREE

Blossom Lessard heard the train whistle as she came out of the marshal's office. The locomotive had arrived early and she'd had firm instructions to be there to meet it. Someone was due with money to deposit at the bank and an escort would be needed. It might seem an odd job for a female but Blossom, despite her fetching hazel-brown eyes, acted more like a tomboy than a girl. She'd been born and reared in the West and had a reputation for being good with a gun.

Normally her pa would be at her side, but Marshal Todd Lessard had left town with a posse of men to investigate a reported incident at Green Gulch ranch.

And it hadn't sounded too good out there.

Too many bad things were happening lately: random vicious attacks on folks who were vulnerable because of their isolated homesteads. The town marshal, Todd Lessard, wanted to get on the trail of the outlaws, known by the name of the Three Fingers Gang, and bring them back to town. Rumour had it that the gang's leader's knife was so sharp he'd managed to cut off two of his own fingers and that was how they'd got their nickname. However the gang had acquired its name, Marshal Todd Lessard was determined to bring them to justice before they could terrorize and kill any more people.

Blossom tucked the plaits of her toffee-coloured hair under a cream hat far too big for her head and mounted her pinto horse. She heard shots in the direction of the station and hurried her horse towards the sounds. The small, muscular steed, agile and fast, galloped off towards the outskirts of town. By the gunsmoke coming from that direction she could see shots being fired from several places and mostly aimed towards the log pen. It didn't take her long to deduce that they were probably being fired at the man she'd come to meet. She pulled the reins to slow her horse, dipped down along its side and hung on tight to the horn of her saddle. She didn't know who was shooting, but she didn't want to be caught in the crossfire. The horse shied as a bullet whizzed past its fetlocks, Blossom lost her grip and thudded to the ground. As she rolled herself towards the log pen a hand reached out and grabbed her.

Jay Kato saw the rider take a fall and roll towards his position. He pulled the door slightly open and, with guns firing between him and his assailants, managed to grab at the rider's jacket and haul the unfortunate in. He looked with surprise at the dark-haired wench lying beside him. He laughed out loud.

'If it isn't little Blossom. There's certainly some strange things happening today.'

Blossom Lessard opened her eyes wide as she heard the voice and looked into the face of someone who, although she'd kept in contact with him, she hadn't seen him for a few years. She had a bit of a crush on him, but she'd never admit it.

'I'm not "little Blossom",' she said. 'I'm grown. And I'm here to help you out.'

'So where's the marshal?'

'Pa's been called out. He had to go after a gang who's terrorizing the neighbourhood.'

'And you've come in place of your pa? Well, ain't that a darn thing.' Jay Kato laughed. 'I'm mighty pleased to be in such safe hands.'

Blossom sat up and brushed the dirt from her dark-brown woollen skirt fashioned into riding-pants. She pushed at the hat, fortunately held fast by a thin leather strap, and covered her now flyaway hair. The pleasure she felt from seeing him again evaporated slightly with his laughter and her full pink lips dropped from a smile to a grimace. Then bullets started to thud into the fabric of the building again; a fountain of wood-chips sprayed over them and they had no more time for bantering.

'I think you need all the friends you can get at the moment,' Blossom said. She drew out a pair of Remington revolvers. 'Fortunately I've brought a few friends with me.'

The pair took up position and fired towards where they thought the shots were coming from. Then it went quiet.

'Do you think they've gone?' Blossom asked.

Kato shook his head. 'They're out there waiting,' he said. He glanced towards the back of the log pen. 'That's too attractive a booty to ignore. They'll keep trying 'til they get hold of it, or I kill them, whichever comes first.'

He said it so matter of factly, that Blossom shivered. Kato realized he wasn't the man she knew any more. He'd changed since he'd left Green River Springs.

As the air cleared of gun smoke and woodchips Kato sat and thought. He knew he needed some plan of action, but for the life of him he wasn't too sure what that should be. As far as he could see he was holed up like a rat in a trap with the added burden of a woman. He thought the wooden slatted seat had given him a pain in the butt, but it wasn't half as bad as the situation he faced now and he wished himself back on the train. He cursed that he'd not been more prepared for a welcoming committee like this, but then this ought to have been a 'secret' trip. Someone wasn't good at keeping secrets and was telling more than they ought. His bags of money had become a magnet for all and sundry.

Kato's thoughts still centred on Duke Heeley, sure that his kin had come gunning for him, but if so he brought a lot of help with him. Kato didn't figure him like that; Heeley would've called him out, not taken pot shots at him.

He looked at Blossom squatting beside him with a gun. The girl was waiting for him to tell her what to do, and whilst sometimes that might be a man's dream, he wished he had a good man by his side instead of someone who might need a nursemaid. If God had wanted to give him a payback, he'd picked a hell of a good time.

'So what you figure we do?' Blossom asked.

Jay Kato, fingers on his lips, shook his head. One thing he did figure was he didn't want the girl making a noise. He moved her nearer the window and with his hands mimicked the action of opening the door and going outside. Blossom pointed to herself. Kato moved his head from side to side and mouthed, 'Stay and cover me,' then yanked open the door and rushed out.

He had no idea how many gunfighters were out there, but he wasn't going to stay here waiting for the enemy to shoot him to bits. He'd be able to see how many he was up against by the gunsmoke from bullets they fired.

So, under the covering fire that Blossom gave him, he focused on these signs, made his way to an overturned wagon and looked round. The pen looked as if a whole army of bears had taken bites out of it and he feared those 'bears' were now waiting to get to the main course: him; and he didn't fancy being on anyone's menu.

He took stock and looked about him. He could make out five points where the shots were coming from. If he could take out a couple it would certainly make the odds better and perhaps make the others reconsider, turn tail and run. It would give him time to get to town and find a better place to hole up. That they would keep trying he had no doubt. The attraction of the money was too strong for him hope that they'd just go away.

Then something caught his attention; someone had managed to get to the roof of the old train and was pointing a shotgun at the log pen door. Kato's stomach lurched. If Blossom Lessard took it into her head to follow him out instead of waiting inside as he'd told her, then she'd get the full blast of both barrels. He started to move his position to take the man out with his rifle.

He needn't have worried. Even though a multi-tude of gunshots had almost shattered her eardrums, it was obvious that Blossom had heard the sound of heavy boots on the carriage roof following a brief lull in the shooting after he'd left. Undaunted and unafraid, he saw her gently nudge the door open and aim her guns upwards in the area where she believed the man to be. She pulled the triggers of both guns and let him have it.

Jay Kato saw her fire, heard the blast of the guns, the bloodcurdling scream, and watched as the body fell from the roof. It wasn't a pretty sight. It looked like the man had taken it through his chest and face. He heard the sound of the thud as his body hit the floor. Kato reckoned there'd be so little left of his smile even his mother wouldn't recognize him. In response a volley was aimed at the pen, but Blossom had taken cover, quickly firing off her shots and disappearing before they had a chance to catch her. They ended up merely peppering the walls with their ammo.

He knew then that he could leave Blossom to look after herself; the girl had proved she could put up a reasonable show. He edged along the over-turned wagon, crawling slowly to a pile of barrels, thankful that whoever was responsible for looking after this place had done a pretty awful job. He used the debris to keep himself hidden.

A shot came from the water tower and that was

where Kato headed. A bullet made a hole through the barrel next to him. He knew he had to shoot the man right out of that perch or he'd be joining what was left of that varmint by the log pen door. He cursed the sun. It had moved across the sky and its glare made it difficult to see the man's position. More bullets followed and tattooed a line of dirt right up to the toe of his leather boot. Luckily for Kato the man in the water tower gave his position away. Kato mentally calculated the angle of fire and blasted in that direction. A scream and the thud of a body hitting the ground told him he'd made a direct hit. If the bullet hadn't killed him then the crunch of broken bones told him the fall had done the rest.

Neither of them had to look for other gunmen because the sound of horses galloping away told him that his attackers weren't staying around to get any more punishment.

For the moment Jay Kato was safe. But he knew he'd have to get to town before they regrouped and started after him again.

# CHAPTER FOUR

'What on earth's been happening around here?' Jay Kato quizzed Blossom.

Together they dragged the two bodies into the pen. They couldn't leave them outside as the flies and the sun made short work of bodies. He didn't care much what happened to them but he gave a thought to the people who had to pick them up to take them to Boot Hill.

He stared at her as he shut the door. 'I only left here five years ago and now this town is crazier than a run-over raccoon.'

Blossom kicked at the dirt with the pointed toe of her black boots, kept her hands deep in the pockets of her leather jacket. Kato remembered her as always having an opinion, but for once she wasn't too keen to voice it. It seemed to be with a kind of reluctance that she eventually spoke.

'Pa is looking forward to retirement,' she said.

Her round hazel eyes said more, but loyal to her pa, her lips were sealed to further information.

Kato understood and tried to make it easier for her.

'So he's finding it hard to keep up with things?'

He could imagine how quickly drifters from the badlands would be attracted to a place where the Marshal wasn't as sharp on the draw as he used to be.

Blossom relaxed; Jay Kato wouldn't badmouth her pa.

'It started about twelve months ago. A couple of cowboys rode in looking for trouble. Normally Pa would've locked them up as soon as they hitched their horses, but he just let them stay. They started fights, shot up the saloon, and you know what? Pa sat in the marshal's office and let them get on with it.' Blossom shut her eyes as if against the vision her words brought back. 'Everyone used to have to leave their guns at the marshal's office, or hang them in the saloon, but that's gone by the board.'

Kato would've liked to give her a friendly hug, but he knew she'd rip his arm off if he tried. A one hundred per cent tomboy, she wouldn't take kindly to being treated like a little girl. And this was a sensitive situation, to be handled with care.

'And your pa's after this gang now?'

'Yes, the Three Finger Gang I told you about. They're a bad lot, Jay. Pa thinks they're the ones who commit all the crimes round here. Rustling cattle, robbing the trains, and worse, they've been attacking isolated farms and ranches. They don't seem to want money from them, 'cause some folk are too poor to give them any, but they take a kind of pleasure in torturing and killing. A ranch hand from Green Gulch came into town and begged for help.'

'Sounds like he ain't lost it completely, then, if he's so willing to go and help,' Kato said.

Blossom smiled at that, pleased because he didn't think ill of her pa.

Jay Kato decided it was no use trying to chase the men who'd dry-gulched him. They could have been this gang Blossom was on about, but they were long gone, leaving nothing but a cloud of dust in their wake. But if it were the Three Finger Gang then they'd certainly return. It made him feel better that Duke Heeley hadn't been part of this attack on him. Now his job was to get the money to the bank so that he could leave.

He had expected to be escorted by the marshal but, under the circumstances, the marshal's daughter would have to do. They loaded and roped Blossom's pinto horse with the four heavy bags he'd been entrusted with from Rock Creek and walked into town. The bags were packed with smaller bags of mostly gold pieces and a few greenbacks. No one cared much for paper money because in the West gold was the only trusted currency.

The reception at the bank was not very friendly. Word of the attempted money snatch had already got to town. When they arrived at the bank, the manager, Elwood Malott, refused to have anything to do with him. Definitely not the sort of welcome you'd expect when loaded up with money. The overweight man, spilling out of a good quality cloth suit that might once have fitted him, fiddled nervously with a pair of wire framed oval spectacles. The centre parting of his grey hair made him look like a rather overstuffed owl.

'I can't keep it here,' he said.

'Never heard of a bank refusing money before,' Jay Kato commented.

'Mister, as soon as those outlaws know the money is here then they'll come looking for it. Marshal Lessard is out of town. I've got my family and my staff to think of.'

'This whole town is going to be overrun with outlaws if you don't stop them.'

'It's not my job to stop them,' Elwood Malott said.

'Its everyone's job to stop lawbreakers.'

'You've got to help these people, Mr Malott.'

They both turned to look at a man who introduced himself to Jay Kato as Abraham Gils. Outwardly he fitted the image of a bank teller: a smooth chin too young for much facial hair, smart fitted jacket, narrow pants, a fob watch chain across his waistcoat, and a tie knotted too tightly over a frayed shirt collar underneath his chin. Yet he bubbled with energy that didn't sit well with a staid bank employee.

Kato could see that the bank manager wasn't too pleased at the young man's interruption. Abraham Gil continued undeterred.

'We've got a safe that could hold that 'til our customers need it.'

'Yes, and we've got gunmen who will kill us trying to get to it first.' Elwood Malott wasn't to be moved by Gils's plea.

Without another word, Jay Kato picked up a couple of the leather bags holding the money and made his way to the door. Blossom did likewise. The young man grabbed his derby hat, which he clamped unceremoniously on his head of wavy dark hair, and fell into step by their sides.

'I'll help you carry those bags, sir, miss.'

He took hold of one of the bags that Blossom was about to carry out. She hesitated, unwilling to let go; however Kato nodded towards her to indicate he had no objections to the help. Then he spoke to the man.

'Thank you.' Jay Kato looked at the eager youngster. 'I'm sure you'll go far in life,' he observed, 'but not as a bank clerk.'

Blossom Lessard, who had stood by his side in the

bank as an extra gun to guard the money, had expected that that would to be the end of her role. However, as Mr Malott refused to help, she suggested that Kato and Abraham Gils should go back to her pa's office.

'It's about the safest place in town,' she said.

'Good as anywhere, I suppose,' Kato answered. 'I'd best go to the Western Union office first and telegraph Wells Fargo that I arrived safely – almost, that is, and that I'll be keeping the money a little longer than expected.'

'I'd like to volunteer to stay and help to guard the money,' Abraham Gils said.

'Can you hold a gun?'

The young man nodded just a little too quickly for Kato's liking but any help was better than none, because the outlaws were sure to be gathering for another go at the gold.

'OK,' said Kato.

Jay Kato knew he had to resign himself to stay a while longer. He had to wait and guard the money until Marshal Lessard returned, because he couldn't leave it with Blossom, no matter how much of a man she reckoned she was, or indeed the young man who, though full of enthusiasm, maybe had little else to offer.

'Nice jail you got here,' Jay Kato said.

The town boasted a strong jail built solidly of schist rock firmly set in mortar. Kato would have said it to be escape-proof but Blossom said Marshal Lessard had insisted on leg irons in the centre of the floor in each of the two cells as extra insurance.

'Pa is always boasting no one would get out of here while he is marshal,' Blossom said.

'Looks as if it ain't been used in a while,' Jay Kato observed. He saw the layers of debris on the floor and cobwebs on the walls.

'Well, we don't go in for spring cleaning around here.' Blossom, defensive of her pa, snapped at the Wells Fargo agent.

Kato held his hands up. 'Sorry,' he said. The four bags were dropped, one by one, in the middle of a cell and the door closed. 'You got a key?' he asked. Blossom nodded. 'Then lock the door. This jail has got a new inmate.'

Blossom, if nothing else was a practical girl.

'I'll get you both some roast chicken and dumplings from our place, just across the street. Could get you a couple of blankets as well,' she said.

Jay Kato shook his head at that suggestion. An hour's respite from the outlaws, that was all they could hope for, and he wanted to be wide awake and waiting. He'd bet those desperadoes wouldn't be resting until they'd got the gold.

'The chicken will do us fine but no one is sleeping until I hand over the money.'

She left to get the victuals and he locked the door

after her. He spent some time checking on the gun cupboard. He gave Abraham Gils a Colt Frontier.

'You know how to use this?' he asked. Gils looked at the object as if it was a toad with six legs. 'You hold it like this and shoot at anyone who tries to come in that we don't like,' Jay Kato explained. He favoured an easy-to-use .40 calibre double-action gun for the boy. 'Feel it,' he said. 'The rubber grip fits in your hand like a glove.'

Abraham Gils blushed. 'I know how to shoot,' he explained. 'It's only that I've never shot at anything but a tin can in the yard before.'

Gils moved the gun around, checking the barrel for bullets, then he snapped it shut.

'Well, you can find out how good you really are now.'

Kato was relieved, however, that at least the youngster knew one end of the gun from the other. He decided his Winchester repeater would suit himself best and he made sure they had plenty of ammo. Then he sat on the marshal's chair with his booted feet on the desk. He didn't look exactly comfortable, but he did look as if he was ready for any trouble that might show up.

He used the time to try and take stock of what had happened to him.

Obviously the outlaws were after his money. Perhaps they'd decided a small-town station was as good a target as any, because he knew that holding up a train is no mean feat to accomplish. They might have succeeded if Blossom Lessard hadn't come to his aid, not that he wanted to admit to a chit of a girl wearing britches instead of a skirt, that she'd saved his bacon. Or at least put an early end to the fight. But he'd thanked her anyway. He believed in praise where it was due.

At first he'd thought it was Duke Heeley taking pot shots at him. However, he'd pushed that line of reasoning away. Something didn't quite fit there. His lips pulled into a snarl at the thought of meeting up with Duke. There was real bad blood between them and Jay Kato wasn't too sure how a meeting between them would pan out. For different reasons they were on opposite sides of the law.

Then there was the gang of outlaws that Todd Lessard was out chasing with a posse.

In fact, when he thought about all the things that were happening at the moment, nothing added up. Three Fingers and his gang out at Green Gulch ranch and then a gang of outlaws trying to snatch the money here – that was a hell of a lot of outlaws for any one place. They had to be the same lot, Kato decided. It made more sense to believe that Three Fingers had lured the marshal out of town to investigate the happenings Green Gulch ranch, taking anyone brave enough to fire a gun, and so leaving the town wide open for them to come and help themselves to the money that Kato had brought in.

There would be no lawman to try and stop their shenanigans.

# CHAPTER FIVE

Suddenly a knock on the door startled him from his reverie. Blossom had returned with enough chicken and dumplings to feed an army. She also had some bottles of beer to wash it down with and plenty of coffee. She placed the provisions on the desk.

'You aiming to fatten us up?' he asked.

Blossom looked at the tall sinewy man and decided he squared up well, all muscle and not one once of extra fat on his body. Then she looked at the other man, Abraham Gils, not as mature in body as Kato but attractive in his tall and scrawny frame. Not enough fat on the two of them to fill a frying pan, she decided. But from the look on her face Kato thought she was pleased she'd had time to tidy herself up since the shoot-out at the station. And it definitely wasn't because of him.

'I had this on the stove for Pa but I'm sure he won't mind me putting you both first. And it looks as if a bit of extra meat on your frames wouldn't hurt,' she commented. Abraham Gils smiled as Blossom blushed at her own outspokenness. 'I . . . I . . . mean you'll need extra energy for fighting.' A slight stammer gave away her embarrassment. 'Anyway, that's not all for you two, is it? I thought I'd get a bit of food as well; we might not be able to get out till Pa comes back if those outlaws try to steal the money again.'

Kato looked up from his coffee at that remark. He'd been thinking that Blossom's coffee was as good as any he'd tasted and he appreciated the drink after all he'd been through. It had been going through Kato's mind about the outlaws trying to get the money, but definitely not about having Blossom around.

'No way. I'm not taking responsibility for you getting hurt. How would I explain that to your pa,' he said. 'Thanks for the food, I'm sure you're a good cook. Guarding money is a man's work. So please get your pretty face out of here.'

Blossom's 'pretty face' turned crimson with anger. 'Don't talk to me like that, Jay Kato,' she said. 'If I hadn't a' turned up, we would've been planting you in Boot Hill right now.'

'I'll concede I might have had more of a fight on my hands. You know I appreciated your help. The attack was unexpected but this time I'm prepared. So,' he placed his large hands on her shoulders and turned her to face the door, 'out you go. And when your pa gets back to town, direct him straight here.'

He acted so swiftly that Blossom Lessard found she was on the other side of the door before she had time to protest. She hammered her fists on the thick wood until she decided she'd hurt more than it ever would. She stamped her feet.

'Don't you come crying for help,' she said. It was a feeble rant but she felt angry because her help wasn't wanted.

He heard her shouts, then the sound of her feet moving away across the boardwalk. He hadn't meant to sound so mean but he couldn't fight a gang of outlaws and worry about her safety at the same time.

Abraham Gils looked at him and blew out his breath. 'You like courting trouble,' he said.

'I know she's as angry as a pup with its tail cut off at the moment, but she'll get over it,' Kato answered.

At least that was his hope as he secured the door with a thick plank of wood slotted into two large brackets and then pulled the wooden shutters closed over the windows. Whoever designed them had been thoughtful enough to make slits to look through or to poke a gun out of. The marshal's office had only one entrance and he moved his chair so that he sat directly opposite it. Abraham Gils sat on the floor under the shutters and away from any chance of direct fire. After making sure they felt safe, they ate enough chicken to satisfy their hunger but not enough to let a full stomach make the pair too dull to fight. Kato drank the beer she'd brought him but only enough to wash the food down his throat and assuage his thirst. Abraham Gils made do with his drink of coffee.

Jay Kato felt a dull ache niggling at his innards. He'd had no chance to take a break since he set out early this morning, so he used the bucket in the cell to piss in, deciding not to do it through a barred window and give someone on the outside something so vital to shoot at. It also drew his attention to the fact that there was another way in, at least a way in with the barrel of a gun: the cell window made him more vulnerable. He wondered why on earth someone who'd broken the law should have had any provision by which they could see daylight at all. Jay Kato moved his chair against the wall where he could see all the windows and the door. He aimed to be ready and waiting when they tried to get the money. He had a gut feeling that they'd be back soon and he was determined to deliver the money to the right people, or die trying.

Blossom kicked her heels for a couple of minutes, then left the marshal's office. Let the darn man, Jay Kato, go hang, she muttered under her breath, and pulled her hat down so far her head almost disap-

peared. She walked down Main Street and wondered whether she wanted to be able to see.
Everywhere looked deserted. Windows and doors
were barred and locked as if everyone had left
town. They all expected trouble and they didn't
want to be a part of it. It angered Blossom that folks
had just turned their backs on the man who'd
arrived in town with money for them to invest in
their lives. It could make a town into a city as it
grew and prospered. They hadn't the guts to stand
and fight the outlaws. Her pa always brooked no
trouble from the drifters and saddle tramps who
drifted into town and perhaps in the past he'd
done such a good job that the townsfolk had given
up their responsibility towards helping keep the
town clean of troublemakers. And more fool them
for doing so, she thought. If the town was in a mess,
the lack of community spirit had surely helped to
turn it that way.

Blossom knew Jay Kato didn't want her help. The
man had always had an independent streak, so she
decided to ignore him and help him out regardless
of what he thought he wanted.

The men who'd attacked him at the station would
only be thwarted for a short time. They'd expected
an easy picking and hadn't bothered too much,
perhaps thinking that with the marshal gone, the
Wells Fargo agent would be only too glad to let the

money go and get himself away unscathed.

How wrong they'd been.

Jay Kato sat quietly waiting for something to happen. The only sounds he could hear came from the Lone Star saloon. He imagined that the outlaws would be stoking up on whiskey, preparing to attack the jail. Like Blossom he realized that the townsfolk weren't willing to help. They had shown a yellow streak when the banker had refused to lock the money in the safe.

He looked at the hands of the wooden clock on the wall, its brass movement was making a decidedly loud noise as the minutes ticked the time away. He supposed the outlaws would wait until dusk, when it would be easy to creep up to the town jail. He didn't light the wick of the oil lamp but allowed the shadows to grow deeper and his eyes slowly to get used to the changing light. He'd travelled around the country during day and night and felt comfortable with both.

'You think they'll be here soon?'

Abraham Gils's voice jolted him out of his reverie.

'Maybe,' he said.

'You're the first one to get this far,' Gils said.

Jay Kato raised one bushy eyebrow.

'What?'

'Seen five others with money. As I said, you're the first one to make it to the bank. Three never made it at all. The others just handed it over at the station.'

'You don't say,' Kato commented.

He seethed inwardly. Putman hadn't been straight with him. He'd know that Kato wouldn't volunteer for a suicide job. Kato had got his own reasons for not wanting to come back here and this job wouldn't have made him change his mind at all.

Both men heard a sound from underneath the barred cell window. A series of cusses broke the silence that had fallen over the town and its jail. Jay Kato, alert to any movement, allowed himself a small smile. Earlier he'd smashed up a couple of bottles of beer and thrown glass out of the window and it sounded as though someone with the idea of creeping up to the jail had removed his boots and just taken a few glass shards in his feet.

Now he knew the fight was about to start.

# CHAPTER SIX

As the sun descended and the shadows set the ranch starkly against the horizon, Todd Lessard and his posse, arrived at Green Gulch ranch.

The posse consisted of Zach Ryan, a young deputy; some brave townsfolk, Miles Willard, Jess Couples and Mort Danes, together with a couple of men from the saloon, dragooned into reluctantly helping out.

It was too late to make any difference to the folks who lived here. The marshal knew it probably would be, but he'd hoped to be in time to save one life at least. When news of an attack at the ranch reached town, Todd Lessard knew the odds were stacked against them.

'Let's load the bodies up and take them back to Green River Springs,' he said. His face now looked as grey as his hair and his brow looked as though extra lines had been chiselled across it. He was more shaken up than he cared to admit. 'The town's undertaker will have a busy week, again.'

No one looked too closely at Jon Tobin, the owner of Green Gulch ranch, his wife Mary, and two young daughters, Bethany and May. They were swiftly carried to the wagon and covered from anyone else's view. Everyone tried not to think that the folks would have used it to go into town for supplies.

Zach Ryan, near fainting, leant by the side of the barn. When he returned his face had lost even the green pallor that had coloured his cheeks when he saw the mess the gang had left behind them. He was too ill to notice that speckles of vomit covered his leather waistcoat. No one else did either. It would sponge clean. However, nothing could sponge away the memories of the things they'd seen this day. Every one of the men was trying to blank out the private hell of his mind and trying not to contemplate what the family had suffered.

'Found three more bodies over yonder,' Jess Couples said. 'They're Jon Tobin's ranch hands.'

'When we catch this gang,' Miles Willard said, 'hanging is gonna be too good for them.'

'We'll follow due process of the law,' Marshal

Todd Lessard said.

'What law? If there'd been a bit more law in this county we might not be here doing this god-awful job.'

The fellow who spoke this last remark, a drunk from the Lone Star saloon who'd sobered up since they came across the murdered corpses, was still witless enough to make the comment. Out of nowhere he felt a crack on his jaw. It came from the marshal's fist. Now the drunk sat on the ground spitting one of his good teeth out of the side of his mouth.

Marshal Todd Lessard rubbed his throbbing hand. 'I hope that hurt you more than it did me.'

'You could've knocked one of my bad teeth out, Marshal,' the fellow grouched.

'He didn't mean anything by it, Marshal,' Mort Danes said. The drunk sat and ruefully ran his tongue over his few remaining teeth as Danes defended him. 'This county is overrun by outlaws.'

Mort Danes stepped back defensively in case the marshal decided to throw a punch in his direction, but none came. Todd Lessard turned away and took a half smoked thin cigar from the pocket of his waistcoat, lit it with the spark from a flint he drew across his metal toecaps, and walked off. He knew the man was right. The county was teeming with renegades and outlaws. This past year he'd not been at the top of his form and word spread. His rickety arthritic frame, and his ticker not running too well, had let him down. And in turn, he had let the people in the town down. He felt too old for the job. But it was still his job and he'd have to do something to restore order again. He vowed to find somebody to fill his boots; trouble was he'd found nobody suitable. And that was why he stayed.

The young deputy, still making puking noises at the sight of the bodies, hadn't got the experience, or the aptitude, to take over. The way he used a gun – well, it looked as if it was the first time he'd cleared leather. As soon as the boy stepped out with a marshal's badge pinned on his coat he'd be drilled full of bullets by everyone who wanted to challenge the new lawman. It was a national sport in the West.

'Let's get back to town,' he said. He threw the cigar butt to the ground and put it out with his heel.

'Ain't we going after the animals who did this?' Jess Couples asked.

Marshal Lessard stroked his chin as he always did when seriously considering a situation.

'I agree we have to find this gang and bring them to justice, but we need to round up an armed posse, at least twenty men, and then go after them. What would we do if we came face to face with them now? By now they've retreated to their hideout and grown in numbers, so we'd be foolish to go after them. You're right; we've got to finish them off. But not yet.'

Again he looked at the substance of this posse. At his deputy, a youngster he'd allowed to bully him into letting him put on a badge, the three townsfolk who'd volunteered to help him out this morning, and two drunks who usually propped up the saloon bar. To be fair, he had to include a marshal far past the age of retirement. It made an inadequate, miserable group standing there. They were not fit to fight anyone.

If Marshal Todd Lessard thought things were bad at Green Gulch ranch it was because he had no idea what was happening in Green River Springs.

Before Jay Kato had time to draw a chuckle on his face at the outlaw jumping around with glass shredding his feet, the shooting started. Shots came so rapidly, making holes across the wooden shutters, that it looked as though either there were a hundred men out there or they all had repeater rifles. Kato surmised the latter. The outlaws were tooled up and increased in numbers, so they weren't going to pull away from the battle this time. He looked towards Abraham Gils and saw the boy giving as good as he got, but Kato feared they wouldn't be able to hold out for too long.

Three Fingers kept his men shooting at the marshal's office. He cursed the fact that the old man had made sure the place was built so well that the bullets ricocheted off without leaving more than chips in the stone. The roof, stoutly boarded over then covered with sod, wouldn't catch fire easily either. They couldn't get near enough to push fireballs through the openings of the shutters or even the barred windows at the back without the risk of being shot, but he deemed that eventually something had to give. He stood and contemplated the wooden door. That could be considered the jailhouse's weakest point.

'Get me that water trough,' he ordered.

A thunderous noise assailed the ears of Kato and Gils. The place seemed to vibrate, and although they knew that the fabric of the building was solid enough to withstand most things, it certainly underlined the serious situation they were in. The outlaws were trying to smash down the door. The wood rattled in its frame but fortunately it wasn't budging one little bit. However Kato didn't know how long it would stand up to that kind of treatment. The only thing in their favour was that the men really weren't too smart. Although they'd surprised him it was plain that they were still plumb weak north of their ears because they'd left themselves exposed. He could pick them off easily. However, when he thrust his Winchester rifle out of the gap in the window and aimed it at the men who held the battering-ram they were better shielded than he'd first supposed. He'd underestimated their resolve. Although the sound of bullets hitting flesh proved he'd hit a few they kept coming at the door. At least one had gone to meet his maker and two more were queuing up to join him. It seemed like he wasn't going to stop them unless they were dead.

Then all went silent.

'Did I hit anyone?'

The kid from the bank might have been good with counting pennies but he had a long way to go on his shooting abilities. He could fire a gun but didn't always hit target. He was no great shakes but his heart was in it.

'You did a good job,' Kato answered.

Jay Kato waited. The gang would have to make the next move because he intended to sit on the money until either help came in the form of the marshal and any men he could command, or he'd take them out one by one.

'Hey dude,' a voice, from a throat that sounded as if it had smoked as many cigars as had ever been produced, screeched at him. 'You stop this game now. Throw us those moneybags and we'll just go away.'

It was spoken as if this was a good sensible idea that he, Jay Kato, really ought to take note of. However there was no way that that was going to happen. They'd have to unwrap his body from it first. It was on his lips to say this but instead he gave them a round of bullets, rearmed and fired another volley of shots into the air. It might be a waste but he wanted them to realize he and the money weren't to be parted.

After the noise and the smoke cleared the voice called out again. 'You'll live to regret treating me, Three Fingers, and my friends like this.'

Jay Kato laughed loudly.

'You mean the gang whose leader is so stupid he cuts off his own fingers?'

This time he had to move from the window as his hail of bullets was returned and zinged across the shutters. Then it was silent. Kato waited for Three Fingers to make the next move.

'You ain't gonna be laughing soon,' the voice said. 'Nobody makes a joke about me and lives long enough to repeat it.'

Jay Kato had been in tight situations before. He'd signed up as a Wells Fargo agent a few years ago because he'd decided that if he was going to keep getting into scrapes then he might as well get paid for it. Trouble seemed to trail after him and even as a youngster he'd be the one who'd got caught out talking in class or got blamed when things happened at home. Truth was he enjoyed a challenge and that wasn't without its pitfalls. As he knelt on the floor, he tried to figure out what to do next; he knew he was in a pit of a situation right now and needed to get out of it.

If the gang outside was the one responsible for

the carnage at the isolated homesteads, then he hoped that that meant Marshal Lessard could be heading back to town. Unless, of course, having been led on a wild-goose chase, they were looking even further afield for the gang.

The more Jay Kato thought about it the more he realized it had been a set-up. The few men with the courage to back up the marshal were out of town when he'd arrived with the money. Someone must have known he'd be here, on that train, on that day. Of course, the marshal knew, and the man from the telegraph office, and really, on that basis, they might as well have put it in the local press, he thought. Perhaps Blossom had chatted about it to a friend over a cup of tea, although when that picture formed in his mind, it dissolved as quickly as it had come. That girl could sure cuss when she was put out over something, but chitchat? Never.

A frown crossed his forehead. She had seen Duke Heeley recently. Perhaps he'd got to know about it then? Heeley was bad but was he that bad that he'd join something like the Three Finger gang?

# CHAPTER SEVEN

Blossom rode out of Green River Springs as fast as her pinto horse would carry her. The naturally heavy beast had powerful hindquarters for sprinting and soon its mistress was heading straight for the marshal and his posse. Its hoofs sparked as they hit the iron rail tracks and carried on out towards the arid plains. Blossom's hat flew off and her hair had unplaited itself again. She didn't care. There were too many important things to worry about, she thought.

Although she struggled with her instinct to stay and add to the firepower, Blossom had left town to get help. She rejected the first idea after thinking it through. Her resolve to go and get help instead increased as she saw them take the water trough and use it as a battering ram. And there was the thought that if she got taken hostage by Three Fingers then Jay Kato would have no choice but to give up the money and she'd have hell to pay when her pa got back to town.

When Marshal Todd Lessard and his posse rode towards Green River Springs the sounds of gunfire came to their ears. They saw a lone rider pounding towards them across the plains, weaving through the sage bushes and juniper shrubs. Lessard's finger tightened round the trigger of his gun. As soon as the rider cried out to them he knew it was his daughter.

'Pa! It's Three Fingers and his gang. They're storming the jail.'

She didn't draw breath as she explained the problems that had beset Jay Kato as soon as he stepped off the train. Marshal Lessard knew there was only so long that the two men could hold up against the gang, and that they had to get back, fast.

He wasn't sure what he'd find when he rode into town. The day had started off like that and now it seemed on course to end that way. His lips were set in a thin, hard line as his hand rested on the ivory grip of his gun. He decided that anyone who caused trouble would answer to its volley of fire. Sometimes it was better to ask questions later.

As Three Fingers heard the sound of horses' hoofs coming up the main street towards them he signalled to his men to get out. He wanted to live and fight another day. He'd lured the marshal and his posse to the Green Gulch ranch but he'd made the mistake of not leaving a few men there to keep them busy. He'd hit town too late to stop the Wells Fargo agent holing up in the marshal's office. He'd been too blasé, expecting him to be as easy as the previous agents who'd been more than willing to hand over the money when faced with a shoot-out.

Now, with his ammo low, he couldn't risk being caught out by the returning lawman. There were only a few of them and that evened up the odds but Three Fingers didn't like any situation where he didn't have the controlling hand. As they rode out, shooting as they left, Three Fingers was only too aware that the whole day had been a big mistake. His men might have agreed with this sentiment but they kept quiet. No one criticized Three Fingers and kept a tongue in his head.


As Marshal Lessard arrived at his office his jaw dropped.

'Well I'll be darned,' he said.

He pushed back his oversized hat and scratched his head. It wasn't what he'd expected to see at all. The building, still intact though standing a little less firm and proud than it used to, showed signs of a battle. Wood splinters from the shutters actually fell to the floor as he sat on his horse and stared. He swung down from his mount just as a hinge from the door fell off. The horse, nervous and skittish, nearly dragged Lessard's foot with its stirrup as it backed away from the boardwalk. Fortunately the marshal held on to the horn of the saddle, his horse's reins firm in his hands, and managed to finish dismounting without ending up on his butt on the floor.

Unsure as to who exactly was inside the building, the marshal shouted for everyone inside to come on out. He held his rifle ready to shoot. He'd seen too much these past twelve hours to go easy on anyone who wanted to cause trouble.

Jay Kato stepped out, his guns purposely left inside the marshal's office, hands held high above his head away from his gunbelt. He didn't want to give Marshal Lessard any reason to shoot before he'd identified himself.

'Hi ya, Marshal Lessard,' he said. 'I'm back in town.'

# CHAPTER EIGHT

Marshal Lessard, less than impressed, looked at the tall man who'd left the town some years ago after a fall-out with his cousin, and watched him slowly lower his hands. Some folks actively disliked Kato for what he'd done but as far as Lessard was concerned he'd never caused him any trouble. Until now.

'I might have known,' he said.

The marshal was in a bad mood. He'd been chasing shadows all day and the wagon, now being drawn up the street, was a testament to his failure to deal with the situation because he hadn't arrived at Green Gulch ranch in time. It made him grouchy and unreasonable.

'Look at what you've done to my jail,' Marshal Lessard said.

'Sorry about that, Marshal.' Jay Kato looked past him to the bodies in the wagon. 'However, that ain't none of my doing.'

'It's all tied up with that money.'

Jay Kato interrupted him. 'I'm doing the job I'm paid for. I think there is more to the lawlessness here than that,' he said.

To those around the marshal, the man's face turning puce made them feel uneasy. From previous experience they were wondering who his fiery temper might land on, but fortunately he took a deep breath and calmed down.

The truth was that Todd Lessard had to agree with Kato.

The Wells Fargo agent wanted to ease the situation, so he looked towards Blossom for help.

'I bet your pa could do with a strong cup of coffee,' he said. 'She makes a good brew, and the best chicken dumplings this side of the tracks.'

Blossom hesitated, then smiled. Ordinarily she'd have taken umbrage at being considered a cook. She liked to be judged as being as good as any pioneering man here in the West. The bank clerk, now standing by Jay Kato, offered to help out her out.

'It's sure thirsty work guarding money and fighting outlaws,' Abraham Gils said, 'and I'd be happy to help you brew some coffee.'

'Thank you,' she said.

Kato caught a look between the two of them. A fleeting softening of her face with a hint of a smile as she responded to the young man. Could he have imagined it or might the tomboy have a thing for the bank clerk? Before Abraham Gils left to help Blossom, Kato introduced him to Lessard.

'This young man stood by my side and held Three Fingers and his gang at bay,' he said.

Clearly Blossom's pa had noticed the look that passed between the youngsters as well because he retorted, 'And now I think he's after my daughter.'

'Had to happen sometime,' Kato agreed.

'Pa, Jay!'

Blossom complained loudly although she couldn't stop her blushing as she and the young man stepped across the street together.

Kato might have appeared to some to be dismissive of the young woman but he didn't want to embarrass Marshal Lessard in front of her, or anyone else. He followed him into the building and watched as the older man sat in his chair.

Lessard had been a lawman for over twenty years. As Jay Kato knew it, Todd Lessard had somehow fallen into that role when calling into town. He'd picked up work here and there, taken a temporary job with a small farm in the vicinity and when that job finished he was at a loose end again.

At that time Green River Springs was a one-horse town, boasting only one saloon, the Lone Star, and that was where he'd called in for a drink after getting his pay. Some ruffians decided to pick a fight with the man with a badge and, by pure luck, so Todd Lessard told folks afterwards, although he didn't expand to say whether this was good or bad luck for him, he helped the lawman dispatch them. Two were killed and the rest rode out of town. He'd only come for a peaceful drink but his fast actions impressed the marshal and he made Lessard his deputy. Six months later the marshal got killed in a less successful shoot-out and Lessard took his place; he packed a gun and wore a badge.

And so that was how, from stopping off for an evening to have a peaceful drink, he ended up staying in the town for twenty years. He married a local woman. They had a daughter, Blossom, but the wife died soon after giving birth to a second, stillborn child. So Lessard brought up Blossom the tomboy alone. It wasn't a choice he made; not many women around, that was all.

Once alone in the marshal's office, Jay Kato decided it was time to do some plain speaking.

'You're not up to the job any more,' he said.

Marshal Lessard stared hard at the other man. The last few years he'd been suffering from poor health, but doing his job, but now he felt resentful towards a young pup who came to town and made ill-considered judgements. The knuckles on his hands gripping the chair were white.

He also felt resentful towards a town that looked to him for protection. These thoughts weren't entirely logical because no one forced him to continue as marshal and more than one person had voiced, albeit not to his face, exactly what Jay Kato had said.

Although no one came and volunteered to take his place, it would have been difficult for a man like Lessard to hand over the reins to someone else. He had a sense of his own importance and standing within the framework of the town. And if he stood down what could he do? Where would he find a man to replace him?

Sometimes he felt he could do nothing but wait for someone to shoot him and then he could go to the place that waits for everyone, Boot Hill.

Until recently he'd been the type of marshal that went and looked for the bad men. He shot first and asked questions later. The town expected this. And it was the way he'd stayed alive doing this job as long as he had.

But now he survived by staying in his office and keeping his head down.

Kato watched the marshal as his face showed the turmoil of emotions within him. He watched him sit down heavily in the chair as if some weakness had overtaken him. Somehow he felt he could under-stand how the marshal found himself in this miserable situation. The pay wasn't anything much, and he probably had no savings. He hadn't said any-thing, but Kato believed the marshal's health was poor. Whatever, it wasn't a good combination;

would he be able to continue for much longer? Perhaps things were going so wrong that the lawman had turned to breaking the law himself. What happened to the money when it didn't reach its destination? Could Lessard be amassing himself a pension, or at least making sure Blossom wouldn't struggle when anything happened to him? Wouldn't it prove a good way to get rich by being in cahoots with the lawbreakers?

Immediately the thoughts started to rattle round in his head Kato knew that he had to find the truth about the marshal's honesty.

'Are we still on the same side?' Kato asked.

The younger man's voice came out deep with concern. A lawman who stepped to the other side of the line was worse than an outlaw. Outlaws did take the job of lawman but at least those who pinned the badge on knew what they were getting.

Lessard raised his body from his chair and swung a punch but Kato reacted swiftly, he knew what to expect when he'd asked the question, and now held the man's wrist to avoid a fight. The marshal's rage gradually subsided and Kato's muscular hand released him as he slowly fell back to sit on the chair again. Now Kato sat down. He wanted to defuse the awkward situation. The two men sat facing each other. Todd Lessard's face had drained of colour. It wasn't even grey now, more a fading outline, and a ghost of a man sat in the chair.

'In this town I'm the boss,' Lessard said. Even to his ears this must have sounded a weak statement. 'I'll have you locked up for your temerity in implying that I'm crooked.'

Jay Kato's hand hadn't seemed to move, yet now it held a gun pointed straight at the marshal. The older man's eyes widened with surprise. Then Kato opened the barrel and let the bullets fall out on to the desk.

'I ain't got nothing against you,' he said, 'but I could've blasted you out of your boots before you'd time to register the gun in my hand.'

'You ain't playing fair,' Lessard protested. 'We were sitting here peaceful like. . . .'

'And I suppose the next man who faces you or wants to take over the town will wait on you finding out he's got a gun drawn?'

Kato let his question about the marshal's honesty go for the present.

'So that's it? You want my job?'

'Hell no, Marshal Lessard. That's the last thing on my mind. But I've got to say what I see. You went off and left the town unguarded when you knew I was due in. Didn't it make you suspicious that you were wanted somewhere else when a Wells Fargo agent was about to step off the train with a lot of money?'

Jay Kato heard the marshal sigh. He hadn't meant to make a speech or to condemn a man who for years had done a good job keeping a town clean enough to let decent folks live free from fear. If he had turned bad, the truth would out eventually.

'I got a message that the people at Green Gulch ranch needed help,' Lessard protested.

'From the few things I've heard, those folks had no chance, even if you'd got there in time. Do you think those men with you would've been a match for Three Fingers? Your deputy looked sicker than a bear that found a beehive still full of bees. The others weren't much better. The outlaws would've wiped the floor with the lot of you.'

Todd Lessard didn't like being challenged. He got up again, so fast that his chair crashed to the floor. He'd been left in no doubt that Jay Kato considered him both incompetent and, worse, a coward.

'I want to see you outside and we'll finish this discussion there.'

Kato was hitting raw nerves with his barbs. The marshal still had a lot of guts but as far as Kato was concerned he'd certainly taken the opportunity to avoid trouble in town today.

'Let's not go that route, sir.' Jay Kato softened his words; he had no fight with Marshal Lessard personally. If he'd done wrong then others would bring him to justice. 'But I think you know you made a bad judgement. One of many.'

Jay Kato belonged to this area, had grown up in

it, and even though it had changed a lot as he'd wandered round the country, he still had a feel for Green River Springs, and everywhere around here. Now he'd got this far, he couldn't leave without trying to put a few things right. And if that meant clearing scum like Three Fingers away himself, and putting a new man in charge if necessary, well so be it. He didn't say those words, he didn't have to, but something deep inside Todd Lessard told him what Kato was thinking as surely as if he'd said it out loud.

The marshal picked up the chair from the floor and sat down again. His colour looked worse and Kato wondered how ill the man could be. It certainly could be the reason for the loss of his grip on the town. He'd like to think it was down to that rather than to his other suspicions.

'I aim to call a town meeting, sir.'

'Over my dead body,' Lessard said.

Jay Kato made no comment and continued by giving his reasons.

'I think folks have got to rally round and defend themselves or soon this place will be as lawless as any new frontier town. The good people will leave and all the scum of the Badlands will take over,' he said.

By the scowl on Marshal Lessard's face, Jay Kato could see this was getting too much. The marshal had no intention of letting a young whippersnapper sit there any longer and tell him what he was going to do with his town. He sat up straight and spoke again, this time in quiet measured tones. At least he meant it that way but it came out opposite and before long he was shouting at the feller.

'I'll take the money to the bank and that Malott will darn well put it in his safe even if I have to shoot him full of holes to get his co-operation. You get yourself out of town, tonight. I don't want to see your face here again.'

The marshal looked like a stick of dynamite about to explode. To defuse the situation, Jay Kato got up and started to leave. He didn't want to be held responsible for the marshal imploding and decided to leave him time to get himself together again. But Lessard wasn't quite finished with Kato. He shouted out as he opened to the door.

'And if you see Duke Heeley, you take him with you. What I been hearing about him lately ain't good. So good riddance to the pair of you.'

Those words stopped Jay Kato in his tracks.

'What do you mean by that?'

'Seems you giving him a taste of what prison is like hasn't had the right effect. Seems he likes the lifestyle and wants to go back. That's if the hangman doesn't get him first.'

The marshal's lips curled upwards in a mixture of pleasure that he'd riled Kato with his distaste for Heeley. At least that's what he admitted to when

Kato grabbed him by the collar of his shirt. Kato quickly came to his senses and remembered the marshal was an sick old man.

'I'm sorry,' he said.

'You're both scum.' Marshal Lessard spat the words out, clearly angry that he'd been treated roughly by the younger man.

Kato stared at the marshal, waiting for him to continue, to explain what he meant. Perhaps Lessard was baiting him, knew there was bad blood between Kato and Heeley and using the knowledge to get back at him. And if the Marshal was lying . . . well he could hardly call him out. But before anything else was said, Kato saw Lessard crumple on to the floor in front of him.

# CHAPTER NINE

Blossom, outside, carrying a tray of mugs, milk and sugar and followed by Abraham Gils with a couple of pots of hot coffee, heard her pa's angry ranting. She came into the room, through the open doorway, in time to see her pa collapse on to the floor.

'What on earth has happened?'

'He's took ill,' Kato said.

For a brief moment Blossom looked frozen with shock. Kato took the tray from her before she dropped it. Then she moved towards her pa's fallen form, ignoring the semi-conscious man's protestations not to make a fuss.

'Someone get the doc,' Kato ordered.

Gils, after putting the coffee pots on the table, did as Kato bid. Then Kato told Ryan, the young deputy who'd had the sense to wait outside the marshal's office when he heard raised voices inside, to stay and guard the money. Kato grasped the marshal under the arms and lifted him up. Blossom held on to his feet and together they carried him across the street to his bed.

Todd Lessard didn't protest too much in the end; he realized his body had taken a step he'd been reluctant to make. At the moment he was out of the action and the only thing he could do was to stop resisting their help. Let them find someone more able to handle the problems that should never have even started to happen, and he would hand over his badge.

When Doc Plaidy had told Lessard he ought to think about quitting, twelve months ago, he ignored the advice. He hadn't wanted to admit that he was no longer up to the job. Now his ticker had other ideas. As he'd stood there blasting Jay Kato for having the cheek to call a meeting, in his town, it played a nasty trick on him. Now he knew Kato was right even if he didn't want to admit it out loud.

'You OK, Pa?'

Lessard became aware of Blossom's voice.

'Just leave me alone, gal,' he said.

Blossom was as contrary as her pa and ignored his protests not to make a fuss. She eased a pillow under his head, loosened his shirt collar, then took off his boots to make him feel comfortable. Although he cussed when she undid his leather gunbelt, the moaning didn't cut any ice with his daughter. Anyway, Doc Plaidy, implacable as Blossom, had little sympathy for his patient's predicament.

'I told you to ease up, Todd,' he said. 'I told you your heart wouldn't last if you didn't rest up. Looks like my advice fell on deaf ears.'

'Pa!' Blossom's gasp of surprise on hearing her pa was so ill, stayed exactly that, a gasp. The look on his face told her he didn't want her two cents' worth of advice on how to live his life, and that his own daughter couldn't treat him like an old woman. For a proud man it was intolerable enough stomaching Kato's accusations and the doc's take on things, only if he admitted it, because it was all true.

Doc Plaidy wasn't as obliging though. 'Do as I told you and find someone else to hand over the reins to. That way you'll have plenty of years left to enjoy. Otherwise. . . .' Doc Plaidy folded his stethoscope into his pocket and left a bottle of pills on the table. 'I'll be telling Ross to stand ready. He's always there to pick up those I can't treat anymore.'

Ross was the town's carpenter and coffin-maker.

Jay Kato filled the silence left by the doc's departure.

'This meeting I want to organize is sensible, Marshal. This town needs galvanizing into action. After all the years you've looked after them, it's about time they pitched in and helped you, and themselves, out.'

Marshal Todd Lessard was stubborn as a bad tempered mule and wouldn't release his hold on his badge immediately.

'You aren't in the army now. This isn't a fort you're defending,' he said.

'We could organize a posse,' Jay Kato explained. He ignored any reference to his spell with the military and continued in a patient manner. 'That might take a bit of time, of course. We'll have to find some suitable fellers and deputize them. Then work out which areas to cover where Three Fingers and his gang might hole up. And while we are out there, that'll leave the town right open for him. Like you did when you left town yesterday. Or, we could stay and fight.'

Todd Lessard's mouth set in a hard firm line. Despite his sickly pallor and the beads of sweat that ran down the furrowed face, he still resisted change. He didn't like handing over control to anyone. He tried to get off the bed and fell back. Blossom tried to wipe his brow with a damp cloth, but he pushed her hand away impatiently. He started to object but Jay Kato cut in, refusing to listen to his protests any more.

'You can't always set things straight. It didn't work out last time. Give me the go ahead to knock these people into shape.'

'They aren't cowardly people,' the marshal said, 'but they're merchants, traders, farmers, storekeepers and their families. They've no stomach or ability to fight the likes of these outlaws. How many do you think would be left alive after a skirmish with Three Fingers and his mob?'

'That's where I think you're wrong, Marshal Lessard,' Jay Kato said, 'They wouldn't be hiding behind wooden doors if they had someone to lead them and a plan to follow. They would fight for what they'd built and worked for.'

'Now you're saying I can't lead them?' Todd Lessard suffered a fit of coughing, and Kato, Blossom and Abraham Gils knew he'd answered the question himself. He conceded defeat. 'All right, you form these people into an army if you can.' He chuckled amidst the coughs, 'Kato's Army. Let's see if you can get rid of this gang once and for all.'

'When you're well you'll be able to wear your badge again,' Kato said.

Lessard's eyes, black and glittering, in a skull that seemed to have shrunk as he fought a battle not only with his illness, but now having to admit that he wasn't up to the job, stared at the people in the room. He opened his mouth as if to rebut what Kato had said, then reconsidered.

A small crack in his façade of hardness opened up.

'At times,' Lessard said hesitantly, 'I've been fearful—'

'A man who feels no fear is a fool, or dead.'

'No, afraid I won't hack it this time,' he said.

Kato touched the brim of his hat to show respect at the older man's honesty.

'It's the way most men feel when they have to put themselves on the line every day,' Kato assured him.

Before they left to go to the town meeting which every one had been invited to, courtesy of the newspaper office printing some leaflets to post round Green River Springs, Kato took Blossom to one side.

'Best warn the women to stay indoors with their children. Things could get bloody when Three Fingers arrives.'

'Don't think you can demote me to a "womanly" role; I can shoot as good as any man,' she said. 'I can't protest much when it's Pa treating me like some two-year-old, but you've no rights over me.'

'You're right,' he admitted. 'I do think of you as that same little girl that was here when I left town.'

'That girl's grown a bit now,' Blossom said.

'I think a young man around here has noticed that,' Kato observed. He looked towards Abraham Gils. Blossom laughed as she answered this remark with a soft punch to his chest. However, both knew the time for levity was brief. 'I just want to know how many enemies I got to fight,' he continued. 'You mentioned something about Duke in your last letter.'

He tapped his top pocket to indicate that he still kept it.

Blossom had known Jay Kato since she was a kid, promised she'd keep in touch when he left town years ago because at twelve she'd been heartbroken to lose him. She hadn't expected him to keep the letters. If anyone had asked she'd have said their relationship wasn't a romance, hell no; he was an old man, twenty-eight years old, but he was like an older brother or an uncle to her. The Lessard and Kato families had known each other since settling in Green River Springs.

'You warned me to stay away, which incidentally is like a red rag to a bull, because Duke Heeley wanted to even the score with me.'

He left out the fact that he had already agreed to deliver the money to Green River Springs before he remembered her letter.

Blossom nodded agreement, both with the fact that perhaps she had invited him to town by telling him not to come, and with the fact that Duke said he intended to get his own back. However Blossom didn't put it quite like that.

'To be fair, I might have exaggerated a mite. I'm sure Duke wouldn't carry out his threat.'

She bit her lip; she could tell she'd said too much. His hand tightened on her arm.

'What threat?'

'That he wanted to make you pay for taking three years of his life,' she said.

'He always was an ornery cuss, I recall.'

Jay Kato liked the youngster. They were cousins with several years to separate them, close nevertheless; but as adults they had gone their own ways, taken different paths. When they met up some time back, Jay Kato didn't like the way Duke Heeley was heading and got tough on him.

A thankless task which divided the town.

# CHAPTER TEN

A short time after the posters had gone up and before the meeting started, Jay Kato sat at the end of Main Street. He had positioned Blossom and Abraham Gils further down the street, on a couple of rooftops where they could see the whole of the town's roads. A naturally suspicious man, he thought there would be those who'd decide there'd be more profit to be made by slinging in their lot with the outlaws.

Sure enough his suspicions were proved justified and three gunslingers who'd been propping up the bar of a saloon earlier that evening were off as soon as they got wind that something was happening. They didn't get far. Jay Kato stood in their path, his Winchester across his body ready to move to fire if necessary.

A gunslinger challenged Kato when his path was blocked.

'No one can stop us riding out of town.'

'Well, normally I'll be the first to agree with you. I don't like anyone restricting my freedom either. This time there are others to consider.'

Kato sensed a movement. A man, standing by the gunslinger who'd faced up to him, released the safety catch of his gun. The man didn't see Kato move but a flash of white light blasted towards him and the hand holding the gun got blown away. The man dropped to the ground and didn't move.

The other two held their hands high so Jay Kato could see they offered no threat.

Blossom and Abraham scuttled down from their vantage points and joined him.

'See anyone else?' he asked.

'Only these varmints,' Blossom said.

'Abraham, help me take these to jail and we'll lock them in the cell next to the money. Blossom, go fetch Doc Plaidy to bandage this feller's hand.'

As Jay Kato hauled the wounded man to his feet he hoped he'd managed to get all the would-be members of Three Fingers's gang under lock and key. He didn't want the gang leader to suspect that there'd be a welcoming committee waiting for him.

Later Kato looked at the motley crew entering the town hall's meeting room and sighed. If the outlaws were going to be routed then it would take a lot more than what he had in front of him. However as the townsfolk shuffled into their seats he remembered Marshal Lessard's comments about the people who lived in the town.

Once the marshal had grudgingly accepted that Jay Kato had the right idea he explained how he felt about 'his people'.

'Look deeper than the surface,' he said. 'They seem a soft bunch, but underneath there is a common factor, toughness. You were right when you said they've worked hard to build the town and establish their livelihoods. They're the true grit of the West.'

Now as they sat with all eyes gazing upon him, Jay Kato knew, after perhaps some initial reluctance, he'd have no trouble whipping them into a force willing to defend what they'd built by damned hard work.

The first thing he had to do was to find out how many guns were in town; the second thing was to find out who could shoot them. There would be an array of pistols; everybody had one for personal protection. However, they'd need rifles and shotguns and plenty of ammunition.

The townsfolk seemed to want to know first why he was here. An undercurrent of resentment flowed through the place because, as one or two commented, unfairly, Jay Kato brought more trouble into Green River Springs than they had had for a long time.

Kato rebutted this quickly, 'From my understanding, Marshal Lessard has been struggling to look after this town and undesirables have drifted in. That ain't got anything to do with me.'

He heard lots of protests but he wasn't here now to worry about whether Marshal Lessard was up to the job, or whether they ought to have helped out more.

That business was for the townsfolk to sort out later.

It wasn't that easy to placate them all. Some weren't satisfied with that explanation. The more cantankerous amongst them demanded to be heard and ask the question that was on many lips. Eventually Jay Kato accepted he couldn't escape it, so he let it roll.

'You left Green River Springs under a cloud. Lots of folks were glad to see you go,' Pete Prince said. His demeanour was that of a quiet, law-abiding man, and one who spoke for a lot of people in the town. Kato recalled him as owning the sign shop, Prince's Place. It wasn't ever short of business in a growing town. Pete paused to allow a few grunts of agreement to die down. 'Now you're back, trouble is here again too.'

'My job, amongst others, is delivering money for investment in this town. And sometimes that job attracts trouble, but I told you I ain't responsible for all of the things that have been happening here. You make up your own mind about the past. I ain't here to apologize.'

Another man stood up. Bert Warner. Kato knew him well. He and his pa had been friends.

'We all got thoughts about how Kato betrayed his own kin, but it's him and Duke Heeley who've got to sort that out,' Bert Warner said, 'and that's a different thing from what's going on here and now. If he can help, then we ought to let him. The town's safety is paramount, not whether two men acted wisely all those years ago.'

Jay Kato gave the meeting ten minutes of noisy debate about him before he stood up and fired his gun in the air. The room went silent.

'If you want I can leave,' he said. 'The trouble might disappear then.'

Everyone knew that wasn't true. The meeting settled down at last.

'No, we need someone to get rid of these outlaws for us.'

It was the voice of the bank manager, Elwood Malott. He didn't want the responsibility of keeping the money safe with Three Fingers and his gang running loose. He wanted a peaceful life, and as he sat in this meeting he wondered why he hadn't become a storekeeper or a farmer instead.

Now the emphasis was off Kato and his cousin, the townsfolk focused on how to overcome their problems. Jay Kato gave them no further opportunity to discuss his past.

'It ain't about me fighting these men for you,' he said. 'You've got to take up guns and help yourselves.'

'How we gonna do that?'

It was a general question that resounded throughout the hall.

'Maybe I can help.'

They all turned round to see a small, wiry feller who introduced himself as Lloyd Braddock. As he walked further into the room to greet Kato the jangling spurs played a tune to everyone's ears. He wore a white Stetson hat and carried a pair of fringed cream hide gloves, which might look rather dandyish on some men but suited him. He still wore the outfit of the cowboy with denim pants, chaps and homespun cotton shirt. He'd tell anyone that they were comfortable enough clothes for him, and why force a body into a wool suit? God made them for sheep.

Square-jawed and clean-shaven Braddock looked tough, as if men crossed him at their peril. Yet Kato knew that this man, through Putman, had asked for his help, so perhaps his reputation wasn't strictly true.

The townsfolk touched their hats in response to his greeting. It looked as though they accorded him a lot of respect.

Braddock and Kato sat down and the cattleman talked. He wanted Kato to know his history and why he needed his help.

'I make my living by providing meat to people in any state in America that wants to buy my beef. Many years ago I made my way West looking for adventure. I didn't have a tail feather left and I was obliged to ride bareback for over seven hundred miles, because I couldn't afford a saddle. Rode all the way from Illinois 'til I found a job when I reached Utah. I became a cowpuncher to earn some money but when I found I got paid in calves I slowly built up my own herd of one hundred and eighty cattle.

'Eventually I decided to go on my own, set up myself as a rancher, and found a place near Green River. I must admit that as I moved my cattle across I joined in the round-up known as "making the gather" – taking strays into my own herd and rebranding them as mine. I didn't feel bad about it. These were strays from herds that the Indians had rustled or cattle that the army had decided they'd take from ranchers "as their rights" without paying a cent. So if any crossed my path I took them and gave them a new home, so to speak.'

The rancher had a hearty infectious laugh and Kato found himself joining in. Listening to the way it was told, Kato felt the feller had every right to mix strays with his own cattle.

'At first I supplied the Indians on the reservations; then I expanded when I persuaded the army that it was easier to purchase cattle rather than "take" them and have the hassle of looking after them. Then I realized there was a market to supply the North and East with the opening of the railway stockyards at Abilene.'

Braddock shook his head as a look of despair clouded his face.

'Now this is where it gets messy,' he continued. 'Everything is starting to come apart. The railway has threatened to reroute the line away from the Green River Springs. From my ranch it would mean another two hundred miles across some pretty desolate country to the nearest station. It would mean loss of cattle and a drop in price for those beasts left at the end because they'd be a lot leaner after the drive.

'This is becoming a rough place, where law-breakers are everywhere you turn and where the marshal has lost control but refuses to admit it.'

Kato admired the breed of businessmen who'd penetrated the inhospitable regions to raise livestock to provide beef to the Americans. Yet Braddock's dreams of building stockyards in Green River Springs seemed at the moment to be remaining as just dreams, with the railways threatening to reroute.

'I've bought up land all over Utah to rent out to other ranchers to graze their cattle before it's shipped out. I stand to lose everything. And so do these good people who profit by the trade.'

Lloyd Braddock went on to explain that he'd tried to fight the gangs who robbed the trains, but hell, he employed cowpunchers, not gunslingers, and attempts to protect his business had proved unsuccessful. It was after the last consignment of much-needed cash disappeared, that he decided to work with Wells Fargo himself. He used his own money as an incentive to find a good man to get the money to its destination.

It wasn't until he actually spoke to Jay Kato that he realized that Brendon Putman had been less than honest with the man. Lloyd Braddock gently tapped Kato on the shoulder with his fringed hide gloves.

'I'll understand, son, if you decide to ride out of town right this minute,' he said. 'These Wells Fargo gents haven't been fair with you.'

Jay Kato didn't think about it at all.

'You're right. They have been dishonest, but I can't leave now. Anyway, helping you is helping the town and this is the only place I feel at home.'

'I can supply you with a couple of men to help,' Braddock offered.

'I appreciate that, sir.' Jay Kato looked around as if to gain permission from the other men in the room. A few nods in his direction gave him the leeway he needed. Everyone in the hall seemed to know that folk were going to move out and that would make it less attractive for investors. It was in no one's interest to let that happen. 'I believe people in this town want to learn how to defend themselves, so if your men could help, it would be welcome.' he said.

They didn't know when Three Fingers would strike; only that he wouldn't be able to miss the opportunity to have a go again. And as far as he and his gang were concerned the only obstacles in the way were Marshal Lessard and Jay Kato. Kato told the townspeople to expect a large number of outlaws to head this way. They'd tried with a few men and been outdone. They wouldn't be looking to fail again. However, they wouldn't reckon on the strength of the opposition they'd face this time.

'Don't try any fancy moves,' Jay Kato warned them. 'One thing I've learned is that the winner of a gunfight is the one who takes his time and aims well. If you can't do that then shoot them in the back if you have to. And,' he added as an after-thought, 'no one goes near the saloon, or any other liquor place, to get whiskey or beer to give them courage. You got to be as sober as a judge to live through this fight.'

In the quietness that followed this remark men looked at one another. It was as if for the first time the realization that they might be killed had occurred to them. The silence remained as they started to shuffle out to find anything suitable for fighting the outlaws.

# CHAPTER ELEVEN

Jay Kato had noticed her at the back of the room earlier in the evening but the business at hand had been too important to interrupt for his own personal reasons.

Two large green eyes fringed with dark lashes, stared at him. Her face, unpainted in a public place, had lost some of its youthful bloom, but then he didn't think he was an oil painting either. The innocence of yesteryear had gone for them both.

Lilly Chester stepped out of the shadows oblivious of the pious, sucked-in breaths of those who remained in the hall. Perhaps they disliked the shiny green satin dress, nipped tight at the middle showing off a tiny waist and rounded hips and displaying legs with a hemline far too short. Kato hardly noticed as the other women kept their husbands away from her and grabbed sleeves and collars to distract them from Lilly's low décolletage.

A green velvet hat nestled in auburn hair.

'Howdy ma'am,' he said.

Kato touched the brim of his hat respectfully in the manner of a man greeting a lady outside a church on Sunday.

'Why hello, Jay Kato. You've hardly changed one little bit,' Lilly said.

'I could say the same about you, Miss Lilly Chester.'

They both knew they lied. Both had changed. Five years was a long time in the harsh environment of the West. She looked more full-blown, but still as beautiful, than he recalled from the time he'd held her in his arms and asked her to be his wife. To his regret she'd certainly given him the mitten for his answer.

He had deeper lines etched in his sun-browned face and minute moon-silver strands touched the edges of his hair by his ears and neck. She remembered how, following a brief affair, he'd seen her as the love of his life. But she was six years older than he, and more sensible too.

Although women who walked the line often married and did well for themselves in a land short of females, Lilly Chester hadn't wanted Jay Kato to wake up one day and regret being tied to a woman past her prime.

Kato had worried about meeting Lilly again. He'd taken her rebuff hard, coming on top of the falling out with Duke Heeley, and he'd gone back to his army regiment and stayed away from Green River Springs. Now, as a Wells Fargo agent, he was starting to meet up with his past again. But Lilly Chester had an easy manner about her, was practised at putting men at their ease, and he relaxed.

'Good to see you again.'

They both said this together. Lilly's lips turned upwards into a delightful grin and the years fell from her as the smile softened her face.

The room had emptied as everyone went about their business of finding their guns. Neither of them noticed.

'Heard you were here,' she said. 'Word gets round fast.'

'I'm sure it does.' He smiled wryly. 'You volunteering to fight?'

A frown crossed his brow; he didn't want women to risk their lives fighting. He forgot that women in the West did just that all the time. They worked with their men every day, in any capacity from the effort of putting a meal on the table to taking up arms to defend their families and their homes.

'Can't help you much at all,' Lilly said. 'These good folk don't want to know girls like us.' She winked conspiratorially as if it was a joke between them. 'Except when they creep to the edge of town. Then we're more to their liking.'

Impulsively he took her in his arms.

'Lilly, you should've married me,' he said.

As before she pushed him gently away.

'You'll find yourself a young virtuous woman and have loads of nippers,' she said.

'I've always wanted you.' He refused to listen to her protests. 'I've got some money saved and after this job I'll have a whole lot more.'

Lilly raised her eyebrows slightly.

'I've been promised a bonus for delivering my cargo,' he explained.

'Folks in this town aren't all as honest as you reckon them to be,' she said. 'I hope you manage to keep this money secure, but I warn you it won't be easy.'

'Lilly, what do you know?' Jay Kato asked. He grasped her in his arms again and held her tightly. She winced slightly at the force of his embrace but this time she didn't pull away. 'Sorry, but everyone has taken a shot at me since I got here. Guess I'm just sensitive.'

'And you'll have more shots at you before they're through I wager,' Lilly said. 'Lots of men 'pillow talk' to my girls. There's someone around here who thinks the town owes him a lot. . . .'

'You Jay Kato?' Two men he hadn't met before walked into the hall. The one who looked like a big loping giant asked the question and Kato's hands lowered towards his guns. 'Lloyd Braddock sent us to help.'

'You got some experience with fighting?' Kato asked.

'We can sort out anything that gets in our way if that's what you mean,' the other man answered.

'Welcome, friend,' said Kato.

Lilly Chester took the opportunity to move away. Silently Kato cursed. He believed Lilly had a lot more information she could tell him.

A little over an hour after the initial meeting the townsfolk reassembled with their weapons. While some grumbled about the late hour, most knew they had little time to spare. Three Fingers wouldn't wait long before he attacked again. This time they would be heavily armed, and there'd be more of them.

The men in the hall now had an array of weapons. They ranged all the way from blunderbusses to Winchester repeater rifles, from derringers to Colt Peacemakers. Every gun known to man and woman appeared in that meeting room. Several looked as if they'd only just had the dust rubbed off them but most would do the job of putting a hole through the outlaws if fired in the right direction.

'So what we gonna do? Line up across the street and shoot 'til they're dead?'

This question came from a young boy enthused with the prospect of shooting people instead of cans.

'Take it easy,' Kato said. 'Although you can stand

right out in the open if you fancy giving them some target practice, son, I think most of us will prefer a more subtle approach.'

The boy reddened at the guffaws of laughter that followed these comments but they soon subsided as Jay Kato introduced the two men from Braddock's corral.

'These men are going to go over things with you. Check your guns. Anything.'

The man introduced as Stig, the one who was the tall loping giant, with dark eyes which had developed a permanent squint after years of sun and the dust from cattle, said, 'I'll tell you all you need to know, then you'll be ready to face Three Fingers and anything he's got to throw at you.'

He had the reassuring look of a man who'd never run from trouble and wasn't going to start now. His narrow shoulders tapered to an even narrower waist but his thighs were muscular from the time spent sitting in the saddle on cattle drives. A belt wrapped round his waist was full of lead, which fitted both his Remington pistols and his Winchester rifle. Stig protected the herds from both white and red rustlers, and now he'd volunteered to protect the town from those who were bent on destroying it.

Grady Hewes, in contrast to Stig, was stout, and on cattle drives always found nearest the chuck wagon. Out on the plains, looking after the herd, he wanted coffee 'you could float a pistol on', and a good portion of pork and beans. Yet there wasn't any fat on his body and only pure muscle adhered to his bones. He was light on his feet and nimble as a cat in a house full of canaries. He could draw fast and accurate and those were skills that didn't always go together. He'd killed a few men in his time but only those who deserved it. His pale-blue eyes took in the men he had to knock into shape within a few hours and for a moment it was plain to see he wondered if it were possible. Grady knew the boss liked Kato, and he liked whoever Braddock liked, so he squared up and got on with the task of making the impossible possible.

Jay Kato split the men gathered in the meeting hall into three groups. That way they'd be given enough space and time to find out their abilities. That was, if they had any to show.

Lilly Chester sent her girls with fresh coffee and beef hunkered with mustard between thick slices of bread to the men at the meeting place. The 'respectable' woman in the town thanked them through thin-lipped smiles as they too handed over their baskets of equally good fare. Whoever provided the feast, it was appreciated and everyone wolfed it down, without a thought or misgivings about whose hands had prepared the hastily organized victuals.

Jay Kato at last concentrated on telling the men where he wanted them placed around the town.

'I want every inch of this town covered by a man with a gun. You men will find the best place is along the roof tops.' He directed these instructions to the men standing with Stig. 'They can't see you but you'll have a good view of them.' He turned towards Grady Hewes. 'They'll head towards the jail so let's have some men covering the alley on either side there.'

He turned to the rest of the men grouped with Abraham Gils. 'Pull some barrels or wagons across the street to cover you. They got to jump over to get at you and it'll make a perfect target if they do.'

'You don't aim to give them a chance,' Stig commented.

'About as much chance as they gave the people they attacked,' Kato said. 'And the ones that we don't kill, we'll hang. So let's get ready.'

Blossom stood there with hands on hips as he turned to leave. She voiced her question again.

'And what about the women of this town?' she asked.

'Just tell 'em to keep out the way,' he said.

Jay Kato didn't wait to hear her retorts but he bet the air would turn blue with the cusses that'd fall from those lips. His mind was on the stationing of men with guns around the town. As he turned away from Blossom he saw Lilly, arms full of left-over food, staring at him. He knew her well enough to realize it was a censorious gaze. It made him uncomfortable, because he'd spoken hastily. Women pioneers had crossed the land with their men, not several paces behind but by their sides. The bad situation they were in, and perhaps an inborn protective instinct, had blinded him to this fact. He tried to soften his words to the woman. Too late, because when he looked again, both Lilly and Blossom were gone.

Kato placed men with grizzled faces and grey hair on the outskirts of town. He shied away from using trigger-happy youngsters who'd fire at the riders as soon as they crossed the rail track into town. He wanted Three Fingers and his comrades with guns pointing at their backs as well as to the front of them. That way they'd have less chance of hightailing it away. He wanted it to be as short a shoot-out as possible.

Hell, more than ever he wanted to get on with his own life, and be on his way.

# CHAPTER TWELVE

Three Fingers, once known as Miguel Camarena, sour and angry from his unsuccessful attack on the station and the jail, wanted the money Wells Fargo had brought to town. Now, almost more than that, he wanted the agent.

Being sour and angry was nothing new – his whole life, thirty long years of it, had been spent in anger. He'd come into the world red with rage, so the story went, because he'd been pushed out too early after his ma had suffered a fall, and he hadn't been ready to be born.

His dirt-poor family moved from Mexico to seek their fortune in the money fields of California, but the bad luck that seemed to follow him continued. It didn't take much to fuel his anger, so it spilled over after they set up home and started to work a claim and the government imposed a foreign miners' tax.

Then a miner said the stake was his and turned up ready to work the claim.

The family tried to fight against what they considered an injustice and took their grievances to the local miners' tribunal. However, they weren't given any credence and the family was ordered to leave within three hours.

The miner who wanted their claim got help to firebomb their home to get them out. Miguel, badly injured in the fire, lost part of his left hand. It also disfigured the left side of his face, taking it down almost to the bone and leaving him without an ear. On the plus side his auditory senses were improved 500 per cent, with hearing perhaps more acute than that of any other living man.

Unfortunately his increased bitterness at the injustice of his plight made him unappreciative of any advantages it might give him to be aware of the approach of enemies from many miles away.

Eventually his family returned to Mexico.

Miguel, however, refused to leave the country and he stayed in the West. Along with other foreign dispossessed miners, he turned to a life of crime. To him there was nothing off limits: cattle rustling, robbery and murder, all fuelled by his anger at life.

To him it was a personal vendetta against everybody.

He got known by the name of Three Fingers, and wore his new name as a badge of honour. He swaggered about in his finery. It was the costume of the *vaqueros* but instead of the rough cloth he had his tailored in fine wools and cotton. He strutted like a peacock in his short woollen pants, which reached to his knees buttoned up, yet open for six inches at the side to show off a pair of long drawers. His feet were encased in short leather boots with spurs. No one commented about his clowning, fearful that he might pull the curved dagger from the scabbard in his fancy garter or pull a gun from the low-slung belt around his hips. He might appear funny but no one laughed at Three Fingers.

Miguel's philosophy began and ended with the idea that he ought to be as rich as everyone else. He thought he'd hit rich when a $20,000 reward was placed on his head. No one was brave enough to tell him he'd have to be dead to draw on his wealth.

Few, however, were brave enough to try to take him on to try and collect it.

Since turning to crime he seemed to possess an inordinate amount of luck and a very accurate aim with his gun. Unfortunately for him his luck started to run out when he tried to take the money Jay Kato was charged with delivering to the bank.

'What you gonna do now boss?' they asked.

To his own men he was a hero; he made them ignore the fact that he strutted like a fool by sharing whatever he possessed with them. It made sure they never turned on him, for why on earth would they trade him in for a miserable $20,000 when their last train robbery had netted them four times as much? And if anyone were foolish enough to think about it he'd shoot the fool down without a qualm. Or they'd turn up with a dozen bullets in the back, and their tongue cut out, as a warning to others.

Three Fingers bit off a chaw of tobacco and considered the matter. It would be a loss of face to give up and find an easier target. He'd misjudged this Wells Fargo agent. He'd thought he'd be frightened off by the attack at the station and, like the other men, be ready to give up without a fight. When they'd used the horse trough as a battering ram after he holed up at the jail it had been like a game. But it had only hardened the Wells Fargo agent's resolve to keep the money. If the man had been on his side, Three Fingers would have admired his tenacity; as things stood he vowed to see him crawl on his hands and knees to beg for his life.

Then of course he'd kill him.

He spat out a fountain of dark-yellow juice before he spoke. 'We'll leave as soon as dawn creeps in, just enough light to see in front of us. That town will be fast asleep and we'll wake them up with a lark.'

Three Fingers hadn't been idle since he'd fled Green River Springs with his tail between his legs. He'd gathered all the hard renegades to his side and would be riding out with forty or more fighting men, all with a bounty on their heads. All of them were good with a gun or a knife and happy to kill for the pleasure of it. They wanted the freedom of the town with booze and girls. A place to make a haven from those who tried to enforce the law.

Paradise.

Two hours before sunrise Three Fingers and his gang mounted their horses and rode stealthily towards the town.

In Green River Springs, nobody slept. Mothers put whiskey and sugar on baby's dummies to make sure they kept quiet, for even the infants sensed the tension in the air and were fretful. Everyone waited for the action to start, as it surely would once the Three Fingers gang rode into town.

Jay Kato moved quietly round and watched for any sign that the gang was on the move. He wondered how the townsmen would cope with the fight. They'd be facing a foe much tougher than they. Men who lived outside the law; men made desperate by the lure of greenbacks and gold. He didn't have to wonder for long. He picked up the sound of horses galloping towards the town.

Three Fingers and his gang were riding in and Kato held his Winchester Yellow Boy ready to fire. He wasn't in the mood to take any prisoners.

Jay Kato correctly calculated the number of men as forty plus, and knew the town would never be able to overpower them in an equal fight. Not that this would ever have been a battle of equals: the men who surrounded Three Fingers were practised with their guns and had no qualms about killing anyone who got in their way. The folks they were about to rob – and slaughter if necessary – weren't cast from the same mould.

The Wells Fargo agent had encouraged everyone to put aside any ideas about turning the other cheek and to follow the Old Testament's teachings of 'an eye for an eye', which would be more apt in the circumstances. He hoped the townspeople would give no quarter to the gang. The reputation of these men was known throughout the country for their barbaric cruelty and that knowledge would be enough to add fuel to the townsfolk's hardening attitude towards them.

The first shot fired wasn't a warning. It was meant to hit a target.

Three Fingers felt the sting of a bullet as it gouged a sliver of flesh from his cheek. As blood sprayed over his fine fancy embroidered shirt he cursed. In the corner of his eye he saw several of his men fall from their horses. His lips set into a scowl. He'd show these people from this apology for a town they couldn't fight Three Fingers and win. His fired the shotgun. The difficulty, of course, was that the riders couldn't see their adversaries. That usually presented no problems because a shotgun did awful things to a man and this one held four shells. To Three Fingers it was a pleasure to use.

However, full of his own importance and confident he could take anything he wanted from these folk, he'd led his men into a trap. Unexpectedly these people were firing back and his men were going down. He'd never had opposition from these soft-bellied, lily-livered weaklings before. He had to revise his opinion of them, fast, for a chance to survive.

'Take cover!'

The order he screamed at his men was the only sensible one to give, but putting the words into action proved nigh impossible.

Three Fingers leaned low in the saddle and tried to take advantage of the cover of his horse gave him. With his legs still in the stirrups as it galloped along the street, he tried to fire his guns towards an unseen enemy. The terrified beast moved as if all the devils from hell were after him, and Three Fingers had to hold on for his life.

A bullet caught the horse in the flank and it stumbled and rolled taking Three Fingers with him. The outlaw kicked the stirrup from his boot and spun his body away to avoid being crushed underneath the horse. Again he used the animal as a screen and fired off as many bullets as were in his gun and rifle, then reloaded and fired again before he felt a bullet stab him like a knife under the ribs. Winded from the blast of the shot he nevertheless continued to fire. His choice, if he had any, was to die with his boots on and his guns blazing.

The street filled with black smoke as guns fired from all directions. Shotguns, rifles, blunderbusses, anything that could fire a missile got used that night. Bags of ammunition were kept ready to refill the guns; the townsfolk weren't about to give up until Three Fingers and his men were down. It got hard to tell what was happening and who'd taken a bullet, but it didn't matter: they were happy to keep firing until told otherwise.

The gunfight seemed to last for ever. Then the call for a ceasefire came from Kato.

'Hold your fire!'

He managed to get his voice heard in a brief lull, which had lasted no more than a split second, but gradually the place went quiet.

'If any outlaw makes a move – shoot him,' he added.

The gunsmoke drifted away on the wind and the townspeople could see the gang lying dead or dying. Three Fingers, sly as a fox going after chickens in a henhouse, slowly raised his gun. He watched as Jay Kato walked into the centre of the street. He believed he might be nearer to his maker than he would care to be, but he'd take the man who'd organized this town, with him. He was so obsessed with killing the Wells Fargo agent that he didn't hear the sound of soft footsteps behind him.

Abraham Gils had taken a leaf out of the outlaw's book and slipped off his boots. He'd moved as quiet as molasses over sand and thrust a gun into Three Fingers's neck.

'Make your choice, Three Fingers,' he said. 'You can die here or wait for the circuit judge.'

Three Fingers put his gun down. He knew he was beaten.

Jay Kato strode over. As he picked up the outlaw's guns he said to Gils, 'I told you that you weren't cut out to be a bank clerk.'

# CHAPTER THIRTEEN

If Jay Kato gave a thought about where Blossom Lessard had got to in the midst of all this trouble, he had his answer when the women from the town walked up from the far end of the street, making the strays from Three Fingers's gang walk in front of them.

Not only the 'respectable' women came: the women from the darker side of the town accompanied them. Lilly Chester had mustered her girls and they were as one with the town fighting off the outlaws.

Twelve very sorry-looking men, poked with kitchen knives and hayforks, stumbled and fell along the road.

'Although you said you didn't want our help, we decided to help anyway,' Blossom said.

'My girls don't want to entertain men like these,' Lilly said.

'And I decided that if my man hadn't the stomach to fight, I'd best do it in his stead,' Mrs Malott said.

Some men looked at the bank manager and chuckled, though none contradicted her words.

'We figured a few of Three Fingers's men might try to creep in or out of town the back way. There's a little pass through the mountains and we made our way there. It's the only blind spot around here, so that's what we decided to keep an eye on. It's rarely used, but known to a few, so we waited, and low and behold it was worth the wait,' Blossom said.

'You get us away from these she-devils,' an outlaw said.

The women ignored him and indeed everyone continued the conversation as though he didn't exist.

'We never heard a shot fired, and some of those men look right battle-scarred,' someone observed.

Ma Jones from the bakery, grinning like a jackass eating cactus, filled them in on the story.

'Had some blueberry jam left over from pies I made yesterday,' she said. 'Thought it was a shame to waste it, so we heated it up again and put it into pots and we hauled it up above the pass and waited for their arrival.'

'You should've heard them holler when we tipped it over their heads!' another woman said.

As the men took up the women's laughter the

outlaws were left writhing in agony from the hot
jam and protested at their treatment. Kato pointed
to the dead bodies on the street. They didn't protest
after that.

'Let's get this lot locked up,' Kato said. 'Far too
many for the jail though,' he added.

'No there ain't,' Blossom said. 'Pa had a cellar
built under the jail floor. Normally we use it for
storage but it's empty now and it'll make a fine
holding pen. Once down there they ain't going to
escape again.'

Jay Kato, together with Stig, Grady Hewes,
Abraham Gils, Deputy Zach Ryan and Mort Danes,
prodded the sorry assortment of outlaws up the
street towards the jail. They had nineteen men to
lock up. The rest they'd bury on Boot Hill. Ross, the
carpenter complained about the number of coffins
he'd have to make, and who was going pay for
them? He also grumbled about all the ground
they'd have to dig to accommodate the coffins. The
general consensus, soon decided, was that one big
hole in the earth would do and then they'd throw
the lot in.

In the marshal's office Three Fingers balked at
going down into what he called 'a pit'.

'We could die through lack of air,' he protested.

'You'll be dying through lack of air soon enough.
You don't get much air into your lungs when we tie
a rope round your neck,' Zach Ryan laughed. 'You

never gave any of those people at Green Gulch no mercy, so why should we care about you?'

The young deputy, who'd seen more than enough when he'd ridden out with Marshal Lessard to the ranch, pushed the outlaw's leader so that he almost fell into the opening of the cellar. Jay Kato grabbed the deputy's arm and pulled him away.

'What you stop me for?' Zach Ryan asked.

'He deserves worse than a rope. We ought to tell folks what we saw and let them have him,' Mort Danes said.

Jay Kato could understand men's fury at what they saw as an injustice to the Tobin family.

'We start meting out our own justice,' Kato said, 'then we become as bad as them. The law will deal with them.'

Mort Danes reluctantly agreed that Kato was right: and there'd been enough bad stuff happening lately. Three Fingers looked at them all from the edge of the cellar. His face had a sneering cocky look to it, as if he didn't think he'd be there too long. As if he had a key in his pocket. Although it was obviously bravado, even Jay Kato would have liked to wipe the smile off the man's face. Three Fingers couldn't hold his tongue even after Kato had shown him some civility by not allowing the deputy and the other man the freedom to give him a hiding.

'Hey, you Jay Kato?' Three Fingers asked. Kato

nodded and the outlaw continued in a mocking tone. 'Yeah, you take care to listen to the Wells Fargo man, after all his cousin, Duke Heeley, was with us. He took the other little gal away from us, a pretty thing about ten years old. I guess he's still enjoying the little lady's company.'

Jay Kato's unclenched right hand caught Three Fingers across the mouth. The outlaw's lips burst as it smacked against them and his two front teeth shattered from the blow. Kato followed through with a chop from his left hand. The lower half of Three Fingers's face looked a mess of blood and spit.

'Is that right, you scum?' Kato asked. 'Are you telling me there's another gal unaccounted for?' The outlaw merely sneered and spat blood at Kato. Kato turned towards the two men. 'Is that true? There's another gal out there?'

Zach Ryan and Mort Danes stood like men woken from a nightmare. There'd been so much to take in that they'd missed the fact that another youngster was missing. Slowly Mort Danes nodded his head.

'Angelina. That's her name. Can't be more than ten years old, I guess.'

Jay Kato turned on Three Fingers. Part of his anger was with the marshal and his men. How could they have missed a young girl like that?

'Now you and I are going to have a few words or I'll toss you in that hole they are getting ready for your dead companions and forget to mention you when the judge comes into town.' He caught the feller by his neckerchief and hauled him to his feet. 'I won't forget what I said before to these men here,' Jay Kato said, 'however, sometimes the law might not mete out quite enough punishment.'

Jay Kato looked like a man with a mission.

Three Fingers was more than happy to co-operate with the ex-army man turned Wells Fargo agent when left alone in a room with him for a short time. He gave him plenty of information about Duke Heeley. According to the outlaw, Kato's cousin had kicked his heels for a while after leaving prison, then he'd got involved with his gang. Apparently he'd found it hard to get work with the stink of prison on him, so he'd looked for another way of obtaining money. He'd informed the gang whenever a consignment of money was due and they'd taken advantage of that information. But Three Fingers didn't know how he'd acquired it. Kato believed him.

As Kato rode out of town, he recalled that Duke Heeley's aversion to a day's toil had started a rift between the two many years ago. Heeley turned to crime but eventually, after a robbery that left one man injured, Kato had taken his cousin to Marshal Lessard and handed him over. He reasoned that to be the best action, before his cousin got involved in murder and it became too late to help him. The decision had split the town in two. Some folks thought it wrong to shop your own kin, while others applauded the action and said that if Duke Heeley's pa had been alive he'd have done the same. The bad atmosphere between the two factions had made it impossible for Kato to remain after Heeley got sent to jail.

Kato thought his cousin would get off lightly when he spoke up for him, and he promised he'd help him mend his ways after he'd paid for his crime. When he got three years hard labour, Duke Heeley and Kato were shocked by the harsh sentence.

Jay Kato headed in the direction of Green Gulch. Somewhere betwixt Green River Springs and the ranch his cousin was hiding away. He shuddered as he thought of what might have happened to the child. And yet he couldn't believe that Duke would have harmed the child. It surely wasn't in his nature. Jay Kato mulled this over in his mind. He felt apprehensive about what he'd find when he caught up with his cousin, because until now he would have said robbery and violence wasn't in Duke's nature either. He knew that it was up to him to bring him in and make him face the consequences.

However this time there'd be no one to put in a good word. There were codes in the West that no one broke and got away with it. And, God help him, Kato feared that his cousin had broken the rules. Duke Heeley would hang from the gallows with the curses of the town in his ears and a one-way ticket to hell.

# CHAPTER FOURTEEN

Duke Heeley felt bad.

Too late he'd grasped the fact that he should never have got mixed up with those varmints. Of course he knew they weren't off on a Sunday picnic but what had happened never ought to have taken place. He thought after feeding them information about the first lot of money, telling the gang about it, that his involvement was finished. He received enough money in return to keep his gambling habits alive. And that was all he'd asked for. But it hadn't stopped there.

Things never worked out how you planned and it had all gone incredibly wrong from the time Three Fingers had the idea to draw the marshal out of town, and 'have some fun' at the same time. An outlaw posing as a cowpoke would be sent to 'raise the alarm', wait until anyone who might give them opposition were heading out, and then a few of them would be able to pick off the Wells Fargo agent and his money at the station.

Blossom Lessard, silly kid that she was, had trusted him with the information about the money. Mostly she rabbitted on about how wonderful Jay Kato was and wouldn't it be the best news ever if he came back? She had this hare-brained notion that he and Kato could make up and be as they were before. He swore he'd never be a friend to someone who'd dragged him in front of the judge and expected him to be grateful for being 'reformed'. He spat in the dirt as he thought about his cousin's actions. Jay Kato should've been a preacher since he was so intent on saving souls. The ones he didn't shoot, that was. His cousin had been a soldier in the army, and now he'd heard that he was a Wells Fargo agent, who probably killed more men than he saved.

A murmur in the corner of the shack he'd holed up in distracted him from his morbid thoughts. The little girl lay on a makeshift bed with only night-mares to disturb her sleep. From the look on her face, when he'd found her hiding in the woodshed as he aired his paunch after witnessing stuff that curled his stomach, he knew the girl had seen too much for her tender years. It reminded him of the time he'd hidden away from all the horror, during an Indian raid, until Pa Kato found him and rescued him.

Duke Heeley knew he couldn't leave her there, so he'd got his horse and taken her away from what would be a terrible fate if Three Fingers and his cronies got hold of her at Green Gulch. Under the cover of darkness he found a shack halfway along the route. He'd played in it as a kid. It had a roof and walls and that was about it, but it was better than staying around for Three Fingers to find them. He used his blankets to make a bed for the girl. Angelina, she told him that was her name, and she looked like an angel with her blonde hair. The kid had crawled straight into the makeshift bed and fallen into a fitful sleep.

He sat looking at her for a while and wondered what sort of life she'd have now. All the kin she'd known were dead in the worst way it could happen; in full sight of her they had been killed without mercy.

He broke open his Colt Peacemaker and reloaded before snapping it shut again. He had a belt full of bullets and he'd need them all if Three Fingers came after him. Yet he really wasn't sure about his next move. The gang aimed to greet the train at Green River Springs and relieve the man of the money. Whatever happened, he thought he'd wait until the child was rested up, then drop her off at the next ranch he came across, and get out of the county before the gang came after him. As they surely would; Three Fingers didn't care for anyone leaving his gang.

For now he pulled the brim of his felt hat over his head and tried to get some shut-eye.

Before the sun appeared, Jay Kato set out to find his kin, Duke Heeley. He told the people in town that he wouldn't be back until he'd accomplished this task. In all the excitement of the previous day and night, no one had realized that a young girl was still missing. It was Blossom who'd confirmed that the Tobin family had three daughters, not two, when she found out how many had been killed at Green Gulch ranch after the outlaw's accusation that Heeley had kidnapped a young girl. No one had thought to check the bodies, what with the marshal taking ill and the deputy all dried and green as a desert lizard. They'd been laid in the coffins and the lids shut.

Kato left the money inside the jail. He discussed it with Todd Lessard, who considered that with all the people guarding Three Fingers and his men, it would be safe enough. It would take a mighty brave or foolish person to steal the money from right out of the jail. Kato said he'd deposit it at the bank as soon as he returned with his kin.

That settled, and with the desperate hope that the child might still be alive, Kato left town. He

couldn't rest until he found out whether Duke
Heeley had really taken the youngster.

At first there were calls for a posse of men to go
and look for her but Kato vetoed the idea. He
wasn't a marshal, but somehow he'd taken on that
role temporarily, and ended up with a badge
pinned to his chest when Todd Lessard had allowed
him to organize 'Kato's Army'.

The marshal had said it disparagingly at first but
when the thing had worked and the town had got
the better of the gang, Kato had gained the older
man's respect. The marshal had even put forward
the idea of Kato taking the job permanently. Kato
quietly refused. Lessard, still supposed to be on his
sickbed, supported Kato when he wanted to go and
find Heeley. He agreed that sometimes things
needed to be sorted out personally.

'Men are needed here to guard the prisoners.
And the money,' he said.

And perhaps because they'd had their fill of
killing for a while there weren't too many objections. It surely was safer to be a storekeeper, even a
bank manager, than to be a marshal. If the life
expectancy of a lawman was short, then Kato mused
that only lawbreakers had a shorter span. He had
every intention that that would be the fate of one
lawbreaker he knew. If he didn't kill Duke Heeley
for his crime, he'd drag him back and let the town
have him.

He sat astride the chestnut quarter horse he'd got from the stables in town; its cream tail swished from side to side in anticipation of the ride, and it shook its long mane excitedly. The moment he'd gathered the reins, swung his leg over and hit the saddle he knew he'd got a good horse. He liked being on horseback, sometimes he felt he'd done far too much travelling on trains and he ought to find something else to do which didn't include sitting on slatted wooden seats for hours.

The horse felt good between his thighs; it was a muscular, hardy beast that loped across the plains with an easy gait. It had bucked when he first mounted it. Bred with a mustang, the horse liked running free, but Kato held on firmly to the reins, his legs tight round its girth, letting it know that it was going only where he wanted it to go. Eventually it settled down and the pair rode on peacefully, on what was turning to a hot, windless day.

To the unpractised eye the ground appeared flat. The heat from the sun hitting the earth gave an illusion of water shimmering and flowing across the plains. That was all it was, an illusion, for man and horse moved over waterless rolling hills and into deep dips as they looked for their quarry.

He rode towards the mountains, all over which were scattered hunting shacks; he'd vowed to search every shack if he had to. Ahead, Jay Kato saw the place he'd instinctively headed for and where he believed he'd find, if not Duke Heeley, then perhaps signs that he'd been here. It nestled in the foothills amongst the spruce pines like a wart on a hog's hide. It was a place he and Heeley had used as a hideout when they were kids, and he'd decided it was as good as any place to start the search.

Kato moved towards it like a ghost through the trees. His water bottle, tied to the horn of his saddle, made a swishing noise as he plodded carefully along the path down towards the shack. The quarter horse picked its trail out carefully amongst the thick carpet of pine needles, taking from its master the knowledge that surprise was of the essence here.

Kato pulled his horse to a gentle halt and swung his frame from the saddle. He loosely tied its reins with a slipknot to a root of a tree, and crept forwards to the ramshackle building. He dropped into a hollow, it didn't take much room for him to hide, and a few inches could conceal a man from view.

Inside Duke Heeley, ill refreshed from his attempt at sleep, stretched, then stood and decided he could wait no longer to move from here. Angelina still slept, albeit restlessly, so he thought he'd get his gear and his horse ready before waking her. They'd had no sustenance, other than beef jerky and a flask of water, which was fine fare for him but he had to get food for the girl.

The place, full of antelope, desert elk, deer, rabbits, coyotes, hawks, eagles and sage grouse, offered an abundance of food. Yet he couldn't leave her to find any game. What would happen if she woke up and found herself alone in this wild place? He couldn't take the risk that she'd wander off and get lost. Her recent experiences had left her vulnerable and afraid.

Alone in the mountains he would have gone hungry until a buck rabbit or deer popped up on the horizon, but he wasn't alone and for once he had to be responsible for someone other than himself. Strangely enough it was a good feeling; he'd spent the last few years thinking of nothing but escaping from the confines of the overcrowded prison and spending more time alone. Now it didn't seem so appealing and he wanted something more in his life. He mentally shook the thoughts away, deciding that any more time spent musing, he'd be crying like a girl.

Kato held back; he wanted to catch Heeley unawares. He was torn with a certain amount of indecision, whether he should run towards the shack and rescue the girl immediately or wait until a time when he could get Heeley alone? Should he be waiting to see which way the cat jumped? He reasoned that if he waited too long then the girl would be dead. A dark shadow flitted over his lined face as, unbidden, the fear that she was already dead crossed his mind, but he brushed it aside as he would a pesky fly.

The answer to his problem about what action to take was made for him. The door opened and his cousin stepped out alone.

He couldn't have mistaken the man. Medium height, medium build, brown hair and watery blue eyes, dressed in plain cotton shirt and denim pants tucked into a pair of black leather boots, he could be anyone in a crowd, but he always held himself with an air of confidence that shouldn't have been there. He had a cocky manner that had almost encouraged fights between the boys as they grew together into manhood. The thought that he, Kato, was jealous popped unbidden into his mind and immediately got pushed out again. Why should Jay Kato be jealous of an upstart who, from the moment he came into his family, could do no wrong in his ma's and pa's eyes?

When Duke Heeley's ma and pa died in an Indian raid, the Kato family took him in and brought him up as their own. The two were close, like brothers, until Heeley got involved with a bad crowd. Kato had often asked why that should be, but someone said bad blood always comes out no matter how many chances a person gets given and Kato had accepted that as truth. Perhaps, Kato reasoned, if his pa hadn't been so soft with Duke as a kid, he might have been pulled back on to the straight and narrow path. Kato had never been allowed to stray.

Jay Kato watched Heeley come out of the doorway and move away from the shack. He waited no longer. His quarry had been given to him on a plate and he made his move. He covered the distance between them in seconds.

Almost as soon as Duke Heeley stepped outside a fist caught him square on the chin. The blow would have knocked the daylights out of most men, but the spell in prison, together with an iron jaw, had toughened him up some and although he fell sideways, he didn't pass out.

'What in the tarnation?'

He cursed as he rolled into a ball and away from another punch.

'I've come to give you the hiding Pa should've given you years ago, Duke Heeley. Prison is a waste of time for someone like you.'

Heeley squinted his eyes and looked at the outline of the man who'd hit him: Jay Kato. For a moment the after-effects of the punch blurred his vision. It didn't blur his thinking, though, and he shouted out at his attacker.

'Jay, what on earth are you doing?'

'I heard from Three Fingers what you did to that girl. Folks have got a name for men like you. I'm going to take you back to Green River Springs to pay for your crime. First though, get to your feet, and take what you deserve from me.'

Duke Heeley staggered to his feet. Only a mush head would volunteer to be beaten by Jay Kato. As boys Heeley always lost when they had a spat and they'd had plenty because Jay never let him forget that he, not Duke, was Ma's and Pa's natural son. Now they were men and this fight was different. The stored-up anger they'd nursed over the years spilt over now. Both had made choices about which path to take in life and ended up on different sides of the law.

This wasn't a merely fight about a girl; it was a confrontation between two cousins.

Duke Heeley wiped a drop of blood from the corner of his mouth and the resulting smear seemed to pull his lips into an ugly grimace. Slowly he raised himself to his feet. He took a look at the face of the man who'd hit him and saw a stranger. He overflowed with rage and reason got pushed away.

'If that's what you want, then who am I to disappoint?'

Jay Kato watched his cousin get to his feet. He knew he'd lost it when he'd vented his rage on Three Fingers but sometimes things happened that made it seem right. Duke Heeley had done God knew what to one of the Tobins' girls from Green Gulch ranch, and as far as Kato was concerned he deserved punishment. He took off his leather gloves, unbuckled his gunbelt, unholstered his guns and threw them all to the ground.

'This is personal between you and me.' He looked down at the guns. 'This makes the fight equal.'

His cousin moved his fingers gingerly over his swelling jaw.

'Equal, you say? You attacked me. If it's equal, stand there and let me take a punch at you.'

Kato held his fists high in answer to this.

'This is as equal as it gets,' he said.

# CHAPTER FIFTEEN

The time for talking over, the men leaned slightly forward at the waists, arms bent and fists clenched ready to fight. The ease with which each took up his stance showed a lifetime of practice. They slowly circled and weighed each other up. Both had play boxed as boys, but they knew this was no game.

Heeley made the first jab but found his fist hitting air as Kato moved to the right to avoid it. Then Kato retaliated with a left and caught Heeley sharply under the ribs. A gasp of air escaped from Heeley, his arms lowered and left his chin unguarded. Kato hit him with his right and almost knocked him to the ground. Heeley felt his legs buckle but, regaining his balance, he managed to escape a follow-up blow and moved away to get a few seconds' time out to get his breath, which now came in short sharp gasps.

Jay Kato, satisfied that his cousin would be easy to

beat, allowed him the moment to gain composure. He wanted the fight to last and to have the satisfaction of slowly beating Heeley to a bloody pulp.

The moment over, Kato stormed towards Heeley and they held on to one another as if they were grizzly bears. They wheeled round, one unwilling to let the other go, and then Heeley wrapped his foot round Kato's ankle to unbalance him, using all his strength to throw him off. There was no let up as they moved round and, wiping the blood from an already cut lip, Heeley got ready to throw another punch. Kato feinted and smashed a right to the other man's chin. It seemed to bounce off and with a shake of his head Heeley refocused his gaze. Kato now found himself on the receiving end.

The pair fought without a pause and for every blow that Heeley landed, Kato came back with two, three, four more. From the look on Heeley's face anyone observing would think his ribs were broken and that inside, every organ had been pummelled individually. Kato saw his cousin's body colour red with the beating he was getting, then go blue and purple as the hiding progressed.

After a while Duke Heeley's face was puffed like a horn toad lizard's and his eyes viewed the world out of narrow slits. He hit out wildly as if not sure where his opponent stood. Kato knew he probably hadn't got a pretty face either but at least he could still see his target.

Duke Heeley swayed on his feet as he took yet another punishing blow. Jay Kato followed through and landed a punch that made the other man reel, and, at last, fall to the floor. Kato went after him but his cousin rolled and Kato found himself chewing dirt.

'You ain't gonna take me in that easy,' Heeley gasped.

He spat out blood with his words. He'd taken everything Kato could throw at him and mentally he prepared to take more. He staggered to his feet and made another stab at his cousin. They pounded each other and although Kato was the stronger, he hadn't fought as many times as his cousin. Duke Heeley had taken a fair amount of joshing from the boys at school, who said that without a real ma and pa he was a bastard. To him, this was like all the other fights he'd been in, and won, to show them no one called him names and got away with it.

He'd sidestepped Kato's fists hundreds of times in fights, including this one, but then he got unlucky. He misjudged the punch that caught him to the chin and he reeled with the force of it. His feet went from underneath him and suddenly he hit the ground in a spin. Although he tried, he felt he'd never get up again.

Jay Kato followed his cousin to the floor. He wanted to hit him again and feel the soft flesh under his knuckles and, even though his cousin lay still, a red mist took reason away.

Kato raised his fist ready to hit Heeley.

'Leave him alone, mister.'

Somewhere in his head, Kato heard a voice.

The mist disappeared and he found himself kneeling over Duke Heeley's inert body. He looked towards the one who'd spoken and got the shock of his life. A young girl, about ten years old, stood at the doorway of the shack. In her hand she held a Colt .44 gun with a fair amount of difficulty. The safety catch was off and her small fingers curled round the trigger. And it was pointing straight at him. Slowly she descended the steps and walked towards the two men.

Jay Kato was in total shock at the sight he hadn't expected to see. He'd thought he'd be carrying a child's dead body back with him. Duke Heeley hadn't hurt the child and he, Kato, felt guilty. He'd not given his cousin a chance to explain but had judged and sentenced him on the word of an outlaw.

'Take it easy,' Jay Kato said.

The child paused at the sound of his voice. She looked as if she was weighing up the situation and wondering what action to take. Convinced the child might be ready to shoot him, he wondered how to persuade her to back off. He feared the Colt could go off without any aid from her as it jumped up and down like popcorn on a hot stove in her small hand.

But she was used to guns by the look of it, like most people in the West. If you needed to use a weapon it didn't matter about accuracy as long as you knew which end to fire.

'You move away from my friend,' she said.

Her friend? Kato wasn't prepared for that. How could a man who'd turned into a monster like Duke Heeley con her into thinking he was any good?

'Don't you realize how bad he is?' Kato asked.

The child, her blonde hair swirling about her face, an ethereal smile on her lips, answered him. She looked like Duke Heeley had when Kato's pa had brought him home that day, lost and afraid. Kato decided that having fanciful thoughts like that meant that he'd spent too long alone. If he got the chance to get out of here alive he vowed to settle down somewhere and build a new life. Both he and Heeley had trodden different paths but neither had achieved anything and neither had anything to offer. The youngster broke into his thoughts.

'Mr Heeley isn't bad. He rescued me from those men that killed . . . my family. Now move away.'

She waved the gun dangerously around in her hands and he did as the girl instructed. He guessed it wasn't the time to argue with an adversary as dangerous as this. He moved off his cousin's body and as he did so the little girl dropped the gun and ran to her 'friend'. Kato went and picked up the gun. He thought it would be best to move what was a

130

dangerous weapon, especially in the hands of an upset child, well out of the reach. Once he'd placed the pistol into the waistband of his pants and strapped his own belt and gun on again, he went back to where the girl kneeled over Duke Heeley.

'Let me help,' he said. She stared at him reproachfully and didn't look as if she trusted him one little bit. So he tried to explain his actions. 'I thought he'd been bad to you.'

'No.' The child began to explain things to him slowly, like she would have done to any idiot. 'Duke helped me escape from the men who. . . .' Here she paused and took a deep breath before continuing: 'we were hiding here until it was safe to move. Duke said he'd take me to the next ranch and they'd be able to let folks in town know where I was.'

Jay Kato admired the youngster. She'd lost her family but was composed enough to give an account of what had happened. Kato thanked his lucky star that he'd not killed his cousin before he'd heard what she'd got to say.

'Look, I won't do anything to hurt him. I promise.'

The child nodded and allowed him to check his cousin over. Duke Heeley, beginning to regain consciousness again, started to hit out with his fists when he saw Kato bending over him. To his mind the fight was still on and he was fighting it to the bitter end.

'It's OK, fight's over,' Kato reassured him. Then he added, 'Why didn't you tell me the girl was OK?'

'I suppose it was something to do with the fist landing on my jaw,' Heeley replied. His hand went to the injury and caused him to flinch. 'And anyway I said I wanted to beat you up for putting me in jail.'

Heeley looked pretty roughed up and Kato wondered if there would ever be any friendship between them again. His cousin raised himself on his elbow and pushed his body to a sitting position, wincing every time he moved.

'So did I win?' Duke Heeley asked.

'I only stopped because your little friend here pointed a gun at me.' Kato laughed. 'Otherwise we'd still be slugging it out, rolling round the hills and plains.'

'I'll finish this fight one day, you big oaf. I ain't letting you say you won more fights than me,' Heeley threatened. He grinned and his split lip caused him pain. 'Ouch,' he added.

'You'll be fine, you big baby,' Kato joked.

He was relieved that his cousin still had a sense of humour and didn't want to start fighting again. Not yet at least.

'Don't think this is over,' Heeley said. 'Once I'm better I'm gonna kick your ass from one side of this county to the other and back again. And then I'll start all over again.'

# CHAPTER SIXTEEN

Jay Kato rode with Duke Heeley back to Green River Springs.

It was a sobering experience for Kato when he saw the townsfolk stop what they were doing and stare at the odd-looking trio. It would have been a different story had he acted rash and got a posse together. Duke Heeley would have been lynched before he got a fair hearing.

As it was they were able to make their way straight to Marshal Lessard's home without any hindrance. Kato handed the youngster over to Blossom's care, then Heeley explained exactly what had happened at Green Gulch ranch.

Heeley didn't gloss over his part in handing over information to the gang. He didn't tell the marshal about his unsuspecting daughter's involvement; no sense in stirring up a lot of trouble.

'I don't know whether the judge will insist you be

tried alongside Three Fingers and his gang, Duke. After all, you were involved to some extent,' Marshal Lessard said.

From those remarks it wasn't clear whether the marshal was willing to overlook Heeley's involvement with the gang. However the town was returning to some sort of normality and Heeley hoped that Lessard would be in a forgiving mood. Kato encouraged the lawman to be lenient.

'Marshal, if Duke hadn't been there, heaven alone knows what would've happened to the child,' he said.

The child, who'd wolfed down a bowl of stew and polished off a mug of milk, now hunted for something to wear from a stock of Blossom's old clothes in another room, which allowed the men to speak freely.

'I saw what they did, so I know exactly the end they had in mind,' Duke Heeley said. 'I hope she goes to a good family.'

A look crossed Duke Heeley's face almost unnoticed, but Lessard and Kato wondered whether his mind had momentarily gone back to the time he'd lost his own folks and Kato's parents had adopted him.

'I'm sure a church couple will love a little girl to bring up as their own,' Marshal Lessard said.

He sounded gruff and he cleared his throat manfully, but everyone in the room couldn't help but feel sorrow at the plight of the child.

'Couldn't we just forget that Duke had any involvement at all?' Kato asked.

Marshal Todd Lessard slowly shook his head from side to side. He said that a part of him agreed with the idea, but common sense decreed that everything should be out in the open with no unanswered questions.

'Best be honest about it, Jay, Duke. Three Fingers is bound to tell the judge about it. Best get in first. Then perhaps you, Duke, can start over with a completely clean slate,' he said. Heeley looked uncomfortable, as if remembering his spell in prison. 'Leave it with me – I'll put the story to the judge.'

They didn't have to wait long. Lessard had ordered a telegram to be sent to the circuit judge as soon as the key had been turned on the cell doors of the jail. Judge Chadwick Wethersfield, wearing as always a funny straw hat to keep the sun from his eyes, blew in with the dust of the Plains in the creases of his clothes. In fact he looked so full of dirt and sand that the women itched to take a beater to his back like they would to a carpet. Of course no one said anything, Wethersfield had a reputation that said he'd have no truck with any confrontation. He had a notion that the only good outlaw was a dead one and to that end he did his best to live up to his principles.

'That sure is a good cup of coffee, Mistress Blossom. For a girl who insists on wearing pants you'd make someone a fine wife,' Judge Wethersfield said.

Blossom, who'd refused to take her hat off, judge or no judge, forced herself to smile and got busy making the supper. Lessard offered to put him up but the judge refused, saying the local hotel would suit him fine, but he stayed for a meal. Blossom couldn't wait to get it cooked, and eaten, so as to let the judge get on his way. The past couple of years, every time he'd come to Green River Springs, he let it be known that Blossom was 'his kinda girl'. Her pa, although sympathetic to her discomfort, told her to find a young man from the town; that way Judge Wethersfield wouldn't be able to assume she was available.

On this visit however the comments about Blossom's suitability to be his bride were few. The judge had a job to do. He wasn't known for his leniency. He could try, convict and then sentence a man in the time it took to read out the charge against the feller.

'How many you got for me to sentence to hang?' he asked.

'We got nineteen men to try,' Blossom said.

She believed people ought to have a fair trial – no matter how bad they were. As if to emphasize the point she dolloped the stew into Judge

136

Wethersfield's bowl, with a satisfying thunk. The judge ignored the tone of her voice, not being one to show concern about female sensibilities, thanked her for the food and started to eat. Considering someone's feelings brought too many complications into the proceedings as far as he was concerned.

'You want to use the saloon this time, Judge Wethersfield?' Lessard asked.

Most times they used Sparks General Stores because it offered more comfort. To everyone, that was except the prisoners, who were handcuffed to the hitching rail outside while their trial proceeded inside with everyone sitting round the stove and drinking the endless supply of coffee.

'That sounds sensible to me, Lessard,' Judge Wethersfield said. 'I'll need a couple of glasses of whiskey to get me through this lot. I think this place Green River Springs is getting large enough to warrant its own courthouse, though. I'd be happy to preside and have the luxury of staying in one place.' His eyes were firmly fixed on Blossom as he said this. He brushed some more trail dirt from his coat. 'Yes. I think I could find a reason to settle here.'

When Todd Lessard broached the problem of Duke Heeley's involvement the judge, with Blossom's tasty stew, a couple of beers and half a bottle of whiskey inside him, felt more in harmony with the world. He decided the boy had been foolish, but he had enough on his plate without trying to punish a feller who'd rescued a child from Three Fingers gang.

'I'll put him under your authority, Lessard. You make sure he don't misbehave again.'

Marshal Lessard was none too pleased with the idea and voiced his objections.

'Doc Plaidy said I've got to look after myself, retire or some such nonsense.'

'Perfect then,' Judge Wethersfield said. 'Make him the new marshal.'

'What about the townsfolk?'

'What about them? You supposedly should have retired a long time ago, they know that but you got any queuing up for the job? No, I didn't think so. Put it to them and get a badge on him. I know Duke Heeley has been on both sides of the law. That could be a good thing in a marshal's job; two viewpoints, so to speak. The West has gone bad, Lessard. I'm a circuit rider and I see it as I go from place to place to sentence the lawbreakers to hang. Criminals have become hardened and depraved and they need someone who can face them down. Someone who'd go after them and shoot them where they stand.'

The judge pulled no punches.

'Someone like you used to be,' he added.

'Duke Heeley puked his guts when he saw what

Three Fingers could do, would've done, if he hadn't rescued that girl,' Todd Lessard said, choosing to ignore the judge's last comment.

'But he did rescue the girl. It's a strange man who doesn't react to the awful things he sees. He could've turned and run. It's in his favor that he didn't think of his own skin, he thought of the child.'

Judge Wethersfield allowed no further argument. It solved two problems at once. He got up from the dining table, thanked his hosts roundly once more as he pushed his straw hat firmly down on his head, then made his way to the door.

As if to underline his opinion, he stopped, hand on door and said, 'Duke Heeley is your man. This is his town, he was born here, lived here all his life apart from the spell in the county jail, and most folks have a grudging respect for their own. He's got enough of a vested interest in the place to keep it safe. And he won't have time to fool around because he'll be too busy making sure others toe the line.'

When the idea got put to Duke Heeley, he was at first reluctant to take on the role as lawman. He eventually accepted the idea when Doc Plaidy, thinking about his patient, and Elwood Malott, desperate to have someone to guard his bank, made an approach to him as representatives from Green River Springs. Gradually it seemed a sensible thing to do and soon Duke Heeley was polishing the badge that, with Todd Lessard's permission, Jay Kato handed to him.

# CHAPTER
# SEVENTEEN

Jay Kato had put aside everything to go after Duke Heeley, but now there remained things to do that he could leave no longer. Whatever else happened, he had to deposit the money at the bank. He'd brought it all the way from Rock Creek to Green River Springs and it still sat in the marshal's office. Kato needed to discharge this duty before he could leave. With this in mind, he determined to go to the bank.

Deputy Zach Ryan sat with his feet up on the desk. Although six foot one inches in his stockinged feet he weighed barely over one hundred pounds, even wringing wet. From his demeanour it was plain to see that Ryan considered himself a big feller. He had yet to learn that skin and bones weren't the total of a man. His rifle lay on the desk. He'd been left the job of watching the outlaws, the ones whom Kato could see in the cells, looked docile and forlorn. They knew they weren't going anywhere other than to a necktie party.

'Looks as if you've made yourself at home, boy,' Kato commented.

The younger man hastily swung his feet down as Kato entered the marshal's office.

'Just settling in,' Ryan said. After acting like a guilty kid, the deputy found his confidence and faced up to Kato. 'I believe Marshal Lessard is retiring and I've a mind to get his job.' Kato arched his eyebrows ever so slightly, but the boy noticed. 'You think I can't do it? Let me tell you I can shoot straight as a die.'

'Very commendable, Deputy,' Kato said. 'However, you're under a misapprehension. Duke Heeley is the new marshal.'

Zach Ryan opened and closed his mouth like a fish pitched on to a riverbank. His face creased with fury and words spilled out.

'That child molester? In charge of Green River Springs?'

It took Jay Kato only one stride to grasp the young deputy by the front of his waistcoat and raise him up so that they were eyeball to eyeball. The younger man's feet no longer touched the floor.

'Careful what you say, or I'll stuff the words, one by one, back down your throat,' Kato said. 'My

142

cousin helped that girl escape the clutches of Three Fingers.'

Zach Ryan, his demeanour saying that he believed the opposite, apologized.

'Sorry Kato, but I heard different.'

He fell over the chair as Kato pushed him backwards.

'If you hear anyone say anything other than what I've told you, best let me know.'

Jay Kato left Ryan sitting on the floor smoothing down his waistcoat and pushing his rumpled shirt back into his waistband. He went to find a man to help him escort the money to the bank. He hadn't asked Ryan, who guarded the prisoners awaiting trial, and he wondered how long that young man would remain deputy now that he had to accept Duke Heeley as marshal.

It didn't take long to find Abraham Gils. He'd left his job at the bank and now looked for work elsewhere. He'd been deputized to help out until another marshal could be appointed, and although, as he explained to Kato, he didn't see himself doing it permanently, he still had no idea what he would do.

'Seems Mr Malott took exception to me supporting you,' he said.

'You'll find something that suits you better,' Kato said. 'Something will turn up because the West is the land of opportunities.'

As if to hammer this point home, he had to lift the sound of his voice over the noise of building works just a few hundred yards away. Abraham Gils turned to look and commented about the venture across the street.

'Yes. Perhaps Mr Sparks will take me on, he's building another store to add to his emporium. He says with the railways more families will come here and he's going to supply them with clothes.'

'Better you than me,' Kato smiled. 'Don't fancy selling a load of ladies' unmentionables.'

Together they went to the marshal's office and collected the bags. Zach Ryan's face puckered like a sheepskin against a hot fire as the men entered the room and he did as little as he could to help. He merely tossed them the key to the gun cupboard, where the bags had been moved to, because the outlaws now occupied the cells.

'I'd forgotten how heavy these bags are. Glad it's only a short walk from here,' Kato commented.

Elwood Malott welcomed them as enthusiastically as before. The bank manager jumped towards the door with amazing briskness when he saw them and tried to close it before they got in. Kato wedged the toe of his boot in the door. His fists itched and he had to stop himself from punching the man on the nose. Forcefully he pushed the door open and went inside.

'Listen, Mr Malott, this belongs in here. I've

dragged it from the station, then to the bank and on to the jailhouse and here again. I've guarded it from robbers, outlaws and anyone else who wanted to part this from me. Now I've brought it back here and this is as far as it's going.'

Jay Kato paused to get his breath. He hated words when actions would do as well, or sometimes better than, to make a point. He could see the bank manager getting ready to disagree with him.

'I understand, Mr Kato, that you've had a bad time of it. But, that said, it is your job. To look after the money.'

Kato stood taller than Malott's rotund figure by a head and a half. Had he been a lesser man in character he might have considered smacking the little man to the ground like an irritating gnat. However, thanks to his cool temperament he once more resisted the temptation to hit him.

'My job is to deliver the money safely. It's your job to accept the money for your investors. The railway company is eager for this town to expand and the trains to be used. It might bring in its own bankers if you find handling the money a problem.'

Kato saw beads of nervous perspiration form in the parting of the little man's hair and drip over the rims of his metal-framed specs. It felt good to know he'd hit a sensitive nerve with the banker.

'Let's not be too hasty, Mr Kato,' he said. 'The problem of the outlaws has been resolved. In fact, my clerks are ready to count the money now.'

The doors were locked and together Kato and Abraham Gils lifted the bags on to the counter. Then they both stood, rifles at the ready, to guard the money.

Kato could hardly bear to wait until it was over. As far as he was concerned, this job had gone on far too long.

It promised to be a bloody time in Green River Springs during the next few days. The judge, not known for his liberal views, vowed to hang all the outlaws as quickly as possible. Kato had had the dubious pleasure of witnessing a mass hanging before. It wasn't a pretty sight and one he'd no wish to see again. Inwardly he shuddered at the scale of things, yet he concurred with the judge that the West was a tough place, full of tough men and tough lessons had to be taught and learnt to make it a good place to live. If it served a purpose, as a warning to others, then he couldn't object to it at all.

As soon as it was all over he'd be off, or maybe he'd seriously consider the strange offer he'd been made. Caught as he mused where he'd go next, Jay Kato was taken aback by the surprised shout from one of the bank clerks.

'This isn't money. It's bits of iron, wood – why, there's even a hammer!'

True enough, Kato pushed his hands through

nothing more valuable than cut off bits from a blacksmith's shop. His face creased in a spasm of anger as it dawned on him that he'd been duped. He turned on his heel and almost crashed through the door.

# CHAPTER EIGHTEEN

Lilly Chester, soberly dressed for the main street, in a plain mid-blue woollen suit, and walking along with Blossom and Angelina, suddenly found herself caught up in a pair of strong arms. When Kato saw who he'd bumped into his face almost gave itself up to a smile. Had it been another place and another time, Kato would have enjoyed the encounter. As it was, he touched his hat apologetically, and explained that he had to be on his way.

'What's the rush?' Lilly asked.

Blossom and Angelina stood to the side of the boardwalk, both aware of the slight impropriety of it all, yet watching to see what happened next. He noticed them and nodded in their direction.

'Ladies,' he said by way of acknowledgement, 'some trouble to sort out.' In a slightly lower voice he continued to speak to Lilly. 'It seems Duke Heeley's not to be trusted at all,' he said. The frown that crossed Lilly's brow reminded Kato of a comment she'd made the other night. 'What did you mean by "not all folks are as honest as you think"?'

'It's probably drunk talk.' She hesitated but Kato held her gaze, not allowing her to avoid his question. 'One of the girls said Zach Ryan was always shooting off at the mouth. I told her he's probably off his mental reservation and to take no notice.'

'What's that?'

'It was only about how he'd had enough of being just a meanly paid deputy, and he was looking at whether he'd be able to help himself to some cash.'

'What cash did he mean?'

Lilly shook her head. 'I suppose reward money. He's been saying it for ages. It don't mean a thing, Jay.'

'I think he had an opportunity. And he took it. Thanks, Lilly.'

Kato placed a light kiss on her brow, which drew a gasp of surprise from her and giggles and laughter from Blossom and Angelina.

'What's that for?' she asked.

'Thanks for not letting me make another mistake,' he said.

Mort Danes sat in the marshal's office this time.

'Where's Zach Ryan?' Kato asked.

'He's been gone over an hour. Said he wanted to get some food, and he must've been hungry

149

because he ran out of here like there were three ways from Sunday.'

Jay Kato looked for the deputy all around town, then he found out via Billy the stable lad that Ryan had headed out south, about two hours previously. Kato's horse, rested from its earlier ride, showed itself eager for another gallop as its nostrils widened and it snorted and whinnied. The animal shook its mane in anticipation as he saddled it up.

Once he'd passed the outskirts of Green River Springs, Kato let the horse have its head. The powerful animal needed no more than a squeeze from his thighs and a light slap with its reins – the signal to get some speed up. He quickly shortened the two hours' lead the deputy had and it wasn't long before he saw a cloud of dust in front of him. He held on to the thought of giving the lad a darn good licking before he took him back. The boy had made a fool of him and he wanted to get even.

Zach Ryan heard the sound of pounding horse's hoofs behind him and started to shake.

However instead of trying to get his now winded nag to hurry up, he merely allowed it to plod forward. Every mile he'd covered had brought with it the realization that he'd made one hell of a mistake. He had over $20,000 in the bag strapped to his saddle and he knew that every one of those dollars made him a target for outlaws, lawmen and probably bounty hunters as well. He also had to contemplate the fact that Jay Kato would never rest until he brought him, and the money, back to Green River Springs.

He'd boasted many times to those girls how he'd get rich one day. It didn't matter what he'd said to the soiled doves who lived under Lilly Chester's protection; the thing was, he'd said it so many times he'd got to believe it. So when he'd seen all that money that fairly glistened, in the marshal's office, he'd decided he'd have to help himself.

At first he convinced himself that he deserved some sort of reward, especially as the coveted job of marshal had been handed on a plate to that jailbird, Duke Heeley. He, Zack Ryan, ought to have got it, not Heeley. And putting his plan into action was easy. The nearby building site, Sparks' Store, provided the ballast to weigh down the moneybag as a substitute for the money. The carrying it out had been the hardest part, especially now Kato was on his tail. It had been a foolhardy thing to do. He knew that now. He gently let the nag slow to a halt. It seemed glad to do so, as if it had had enough of carrying a load along. It was the only horse he'd been able to afford, which seemed laughable given that he had a bag full of dollars. Ryan had given ten dollars for the broken-down nag because he'd been scared to offer more and risk letting on to the stable hand that he'd suddenly come into some wealth.

He'd have been paying a hundred times more than that if the man had known and would probably have been turned in by the time he reached the edge of town. As it was he hadn't got very far with this horse. He felt that his feet were nigh on dragging along the floor and he slowed down, with the nag's back bowed with the weight of its burden.

'Get down off that horse, Zach Ryan.' The deep tones of Jay Kato boomed at him. 'Unbuckle your belt carefully and let it fall to the ground. Don't do anything that you might regret because I got my Colt pistol pointed straight at you.'

Ryan shuddered as he did exactly as the man told him. He feared Kato would shoot him in the back anyway. No one would know what had happened out here in the middle of nowhere. It would be Kato's word against a dead thief. Kato would get praised for bringing back the townsfolk's money.

Jay Kato looked at the dispirited youth. The boy had slowed down as soon as he'd heard him, wise enough to know he'd met his match, although he was probably wishing now that he'd been wise enough in the first place to leave the money in the marshal's office.

He watched as the kid shucked off his belt and got off his horse.

'I didn't mean anything by this, Kato,' Ryan said. 'It was a fool thing to do.'

'You'll have plenty of time to reflect on that when

the judge sentences you for robbery.'

'Chadwick Wethersfield? The hanging judge? You ain't gonna haul me in front of him?'

The boy swallowed hard. Kato was philosophical.

'You do the crime, you got to take the punishment.'

Ryan nodded in agreement. Kato had been fired up with the thought of giving him a hiding but the boy now seemed bitterly to regret his rash behaviour and the swagger had left him. He made a decision and he took the boy's horse by its reins.

'You get walking now,' he said. 'This old horse needs a rest.'

Zach Ryan's face looked incredulous.

'It's fifteen miles back to town,' he said.

'Yes,' Kato agreed, 'you figured it out about right. And if you blubber, I'll take your boots off you.'

The boy shut up. He had no doubt that Kato meant every word he said. He turned and walked in front of the man and the two horses, back into town. As the two men drew near some people turned to stare but soon went about their own business. Folks were too busy getting ready for a mass hanging to worry about anything else. And they were getting used to all the odd things that had been happening around them lately.

As Ryan nursed his blisters, Kato, Heeley and Lessard came together to discuss the situation. Kato handcuffed him to the hitching rail outside the marshal's house. Kato asked the other two men what action they wanted to take.

'As I see it,' he said, 'the kid's made a bad mistake.' Heeley didn't argue. He knew too well that youth and stupidity often went hand in hand. 'I took the bag to the bank, I explained there'd been a mix-up and as far as everyone's concerned I got a receipt to show I handed over one hundred thousand dollars.'

Todd Lessard scratched his head. 'Really this ain't got anything to do with me. By rights he ought to be locked up with the other outlaws. But it's up to Duke to have the last word.'

Heeley looked concerned. 'That Judge Wethersfield will string him up with the rest of them,' he said. 'He's already been generous, though, so perhaps if I offer to take him under my wing and keep him on as my deputy. . . ?'

Jay Kato nodded in agreement.

'OK with you, Lessard?' Heeley asked.

The old marshal shrugged his shoulders. 'Well, I suppose Kato has taught him a hard enough lesson.' He looked at Heeley. 'It's your responsibility now. Best let him put his feet in a bucket of cold water now though.'

Duke Heeley grinned as he went out the door to release the 'prisoner'.

# CHAPTER NINETEEN

Although Jay Kato didn't have a mind to stay around for the hangings he accepted that he had to give formal testimony to the judge. On the other hand it gave him plenty of time to decide what to do about his future. Lloyd Braddock had paid him his bonus and made a few suggestions that were worth consideration.

He was also pleased that Braddock had wired Putman and told him not to expect the extra money. Braddock didn't mind a man turning a profit but he liked them to be upfront about it.

Jay Kato also had some reward money. It was part of the town's bounty for capturing the outlaws. Kato banked his share to give to Angelina Tobin. He'd make sure she had a good future.

In the meantime he took up an invitation for supper at with Todd and Blossom Lessard, partly to pass the time, but also because Blossom was a good cook.

'Well, don't you look pretty,' he said.

Jay Kato, surprised to find his hostess in a cream and yellow dress, could only find a few words to express how good she looked. The yellow pattern set off her hazel eyes and complemented her dark hair, which for once wasn't hidden under a hat. His surprise increased when he saw Abraham Gil standing at her side.

'We're engaged to be married,' Gil explained.

Somehow Kato had never imagined it but he supposed it had to happen one day when Blossom would emerge as a woman from being a tomboy. Nevertheless he bet Abraham Gil had taken on a mighty big handful. Kato couldn't imagine Blossom being content with sewing and cake making and before the evening was over he said exactly that to the pair of them.

'You're right,' Blossom agreed. 'I can't see it myself. I aim to include a few other things in my life.' She stopped and corrected herself. 'I mean in our life.'

'You know my job at the bank is over,' Abraham said, 'so we're looking for our own place, a homestead.'

After supper, when Todd was out on the porch smoking a cigar and Kato sat nursing another mug of coffee, Blossom told him of her invitation to her pa to come and live with them and at her disappointment when he'd refused.

'Can you convince him I'm right?' Blossom asked.

'Ain't rightly my job to interfere,' Kato said. 'I suppose your pa wants you to make your own way now. And it could be he wants to sit on a porch or in Sparks' Stores with his feet on the wood stove, smoking and jawing and drinking stewed coffee all day. Don't sound too bad a life, eh?'

Like most children, Blossom hadn't thought of things from her pa's perspective.

'I suppose you're right, more than right,' she said. 'Trying to do my best for him and interfering as usual. And what about you, Jay, you got any plans?'

'Mulling over a few things, that's all,' he said.

Blossom raised her eyebrows quizzically.

'A suggestion from Lloyd Braddock, about buying the Tobins' place,' Kato said.

She seemed horrified at this. 'After everything that happened there?' Blossom asked. 'Ought to raze it to the ground.'

'I got to go with that,' Abraham Gils agreed.

'The *place* isn't evil,' Jay Kato reminded them. 'Only the gang who murdered the Tobin family.' He sat forward in his chair. 'Look at it my way. The Tobin family worked hard at that ranch. Had a nice little outfit building up there. They'd hate to see it destroyed because of the evil doings of Three Fingers. Lloyd Braddock said to offer to buy it from

Angelina Tobin. The money will mean a family will have some money to help raise her. And there's land around the ranch to buy so if she wanted to move back later, I'd have enough space to stay there too.'

If Blossom had any other reservations she held her tongue. It seemed as if Kato had been thinking the whole thing through carefully. Angelina Tobin wasn't there to have any sort of opinion and anyway Kato thought she'd be too young to give it a rightful consideration. It did spark his curiosity as to where the girl was though.

'You found a family to take her?' he asked.

'There's a few people who showed interest, but I think the child will need a little extra care to get over what's happened. There's times when she seems so distraught,' Blossom said. 'Miss Lilly Chester has taken her for a ride out in the buggy this afternoon. I think she's taken a shine to the little 'un.'

'Now there's a lady I want to see.'

Blossom couldn't resist asking why.

'Unfinished business.'

It was all he'd say on his reasons but he asked if they knew when she'd return.

'She'll be back here with Angelina any time soon,' Blossom said. 'You want to wait here for her?'

'I'll find her in my own time, thanks,' he said.

Kato hadn't spoken to Lilly since they'd literally

bumped into each other when he'd run out of the bank. So after he'd taken his leave of Todd, Blossom and Abraham, he was pleased to see her driving back into town thirty minutes later. Simply dressed in a brown-velvet jacket trimmed with cream and a plain skirt, she was the picture of a demure lady, especially with her hair pinned up beneath a bonnet, Jay Kato thought.

He watched as she brought the horse to a halt in front of the Lessard place, and hitched the wagon to the post. He saw that the youngster and Lilly were quite attached as the little girl flung her arms around the older woman's neck. He heard Lilly coax her into leaving her side with the promise of another drive out tomorrow. Lilly looked sad as the door closed on Angelina. He watched as she climbed back into the buggy and then went over to greet her. He asked about the outing.

'Angelina loved it. She wanted to come out with me again. Mustn't get carried away though,' Lilly said. She took a handkerchief from her reticule and dabbed a tear away from her eyes. 'Can't allow myself to get too emotional. Another couple of years and she'll be aware enough to know to cross the street when she sees me.'

'Don't do yourself down, Lilly Chester; you're as good as any other woman in this town,' Jay Kato said. 'And a far better dancer than any of them.'

She smiled at the compliment and invited him to

sit beside her. He climbed in the buggy, took the reins and headed back to Lilly's place.

'You'll be off soon, Jay?' she asked.

'I'm planning to stay here. Got somewhere I intend to buy. The Tobin place. If things are right, that is.'

She didn't flinch when he told the name of the ranch. Lilly was made of stern stuff.

'Sounds good,' she said. 'What has to be right?'

He looked into the eyes of the woman he'd left when she refused to marry him. He decided right then that it wasn't going to happen again.

'Marry me, Lilly,' he said.

'You asking me?'

'No. I'm telling you. It's called starting as I mean to go on. I should've done that the last time,' he said.

'I was a fool to refuse,' Lilly said. She placed a glove hand on his. 'Can I ask you one thing?'

Jay Kato nodded.

'Can we give Angelina a home? I've got mighty close to her the past week.'

'That could be the start of our family. Let's go and tell her all about our plans,' Kato suggested.